Maitland Public Library
501 S. Maitland Ave
Maitland, Fl 32751
(407) 647-7700

PERPETUAL CHECK

RICH WALLACE

PERPETUAL CHECK

ALFRED A. KNOPF

NEW YORK

THIS IS A BORZOI BOOK PUBLISHED BY ALFRED A. KNOPF

All rights reserved. Published in the United States by Alfred A. Knopf, an imprint of Random House Children's Books, a division of Random House, Inc., New York.

Knopf, Borzoi Books, and the colophon are registered trademarks of Random House, Inc.

Visit us on the Web! www.randomhouse.com/teens

Educators and librarians, for a variety of teaching tools, visit us at
www.randomhouse.com/teachers

Library of Congress Cataloging-in-Publication Data
Wallace, Rich.
Perpetual check / Rich Wallace. — 1st ed.
p.   cm.
Summary: Brothers Zeke and Randy participate in an important chess tournament, playing against each other while also trying to deal with their father's intensely competitive tendencies.
ISBN 978-0-375-84058-6 (trade) — ISBN 978-0-375-94058-3 (lib. bdg.)
[1. Fathers and sons—Fiction. 2. Brothers—Fiction. 3. Chess—Fiction. 4. Competition (Psychology)—Fiction.] I. Title.
PZ7.W15877Pe 2009
[Fic]—dc22
2008004159

The text of this book is set in 11.5-point Goudy.

Printed in the United States of America

February 2009

10 9 8 7 6 5 4 3 2 1

First Edition

For Jonathan and Jeremy

PERPETUAL CHECK

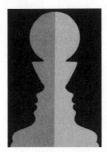

■ ONE ■
Several Moves Ahead

They're barefoot, moving silently along the carpeted hallway, searching for some clue to which hotel room might be Jenna McNulty's.

217? 219? All of the doors look the same. What were they expecting to tip them off? Some definitive prep-school snore?

Pramod puts a finger to his lips—*Like I don't know enough to be quiet*, Zeke thinks—and kneels by a room-service tray someone had shoved into the hall. He lifts a silver-colored cover to reveal a sprig of parsley swimming in a congealed smear of steak grease and blood at the edge of the plate. He sticks his tongue from his open mouth and grimaces.

There's a half-full bottle of Heineken on the tray, recapped and upright. Pramod carefully puts two long, nimble fingers on the neck and raises it from the tray.

Zeke gives him a look that says, *No way you're drinking that.*

Pramod walks—with the beer—a few feet away, so he's equidistant between the doors of rooms 219 and 221. He leans against the pale striped wallpaper and motions Zeke over.

"He didn't drink from the bottle," he whispers.

"Who didn't?"

"Whoever's in that room." He points to the tray. "He used a glass, see?"

There's a clear drinking glass on the tray with an obvious trace of dried beer foam. In other words, the bottle holds untouched Heineken. Warm, certainly, and probably flat.

Pramod checks to make sure the cap is on tight, then puts the bottle in the pocket of his loose green gym shorts and starts walking toward the elevators. His T-shirt says JESUIT LACROSSE, and his straight black hair is badly mussed.

Zeke checks his watch. It's 1:09 a.m. The Round of 16 starts in less than eight hours.

The elevator floor is cool on their bare feet, and it takes a long time for the numbers to change from 2 to 3 to 4. They stop and the door opens and they walk along the hallway. Pramod takes his room key (actually, it's more like a credit card), opens the door, and they go in. Zeke reaches into his own pocket quickly and fishes around, then pulls out his empty hand.

Pramod unwraps two plastic hotel cups by the sink and pours about three ounces of beer into each. He drinks his in one swig and stands there waiting for Zeke to empty his.

"Tastes like crap when it's warm," Pramod says.

"It's better cold?" Zeke immediately realizes that he's tipped his hand.

Pramod smirks. "Much better."

"I mean, I never had Heineken before. I usually drink other brands."

Pramod rolls his eyes. "Like apple juice?"

"Sometimes. Or vodka." Zeke's never even tasted vodka.

"You bring any with you?"

"No. I forgot."

"Sure you did."

When Zeke was six, his father decided that he was smart enough to learn to play chess. He didn't go easy on him. After about two weeks of getting his butt kicked, Zeke asked, "Dad, when do you think I'll be able to beat you?"

Mr. Mansfield smiled and rubbed the whiskers on his chin. "Well, Ace," he said, "if you keep learning and working at it, I think you'll probably be giving me a good game by the time you're fourteen or fifteen."

Three days later, Zeke got lucky and beat him. Soon after that, it wasn't luck at all. He was simply better than his dad. He had the ability to plan several moves ahead. His father didn't.

Zeke always found it amusing that he could regularly beat someone so much older than he was. Until the same thing started happening to him.

Last year, Zeke was the top-ranked player on his high school chess team. You won't hear him bragging to his friends about it. He doesn't use it to try to pick up girls. He doesn't have a letterman's jacket with an embroidered rook or a bishop sewn onto the sleeve.

But he likes the game and he's good at it, and the competitive chess season is basically all winter, fitting between his other sports of soccer and tennis.

The problem for Zeke is "my fat-ass little brother, Randy."

Randy is a freshman, so he's on the team this year. And he beats Zeke nine times out of ten. So that was the end of Zeke's top ranking.

The poker game had lasted about two hours, then a bunch of them roamed the halls for the rest of the evening. Just Zeke and Pramod were left by midnight.

Zeke's not surprised to see a chessboard on the table near the window in Pramod's room, set up as if in midgame. Most of these chess guys are constantly reviewing moves and tactics, reading about it, playing it online, practicing their openings and attacks over and over.

Zeke boned up a little this past week, but he usually doesn't even think about chess except when he's got a match. There's a lot on the line this weekend, though.

They're at the Lackawanna Station Hotel in Scranton for the Northeast Regional of the Pennsylvania High School Chess Championships. Sixty-four players got invited here, and they played two rounds earlier tonight, leaving sixteen to decide the regional title tomorrow. They gave the sixteen who advanced free dinner and rooms.

The regional winner gets a thousand-dollar scholarship. The overall state champion—to be decided next weekend in

Philly among the eight regional champions and runners-up—
gets five thousand.

"We never did figure out which room was hers," Pramod
says, taking a seat on the edge of his bed.

"Who?" Zeke asks, though he knows Pramod is referring to
Jenna McNulty. She's the top seed in the tournament and also
the best-looking player, by far. And she knows it. About both
things.

"Right. Like you don't know who I'm talking about,"
Pramod says. "You stared at her between every move tonight."

"And you didn't?"

"We *all* did. That's why she's so hard to beat. Instead of
concentrating on our chess moves, we're dreaming about what
other moves we could be putting on her."

Zeke's face gets a little flushed, and he nods. If he wins his
first match in the morning, he'll be playing against Jenna in
the quarterfinals.

Earlier that night, Zeke forced a stalemate in his first game
against a guy from Carbondale but beat him quickly in the rematch. And his second-round game was over in about five
minutes.

His little brother, Randy, won both of his matches easily.
Randy's ranked fifth overall. The tournament officials seeded
the top eight based on their computer ratings, and the rest of
the players were plugged into the brackets at random.

It's set up like a basketball tournament. If there were no up-
sets in the early rounds, then the quarterfinals would have the
first seed against the eighth, second versus seventh, third
against sixth, and fourth versus fifth. But a couple of ranked
players have already been knocked out.

"You nervous?" Pramod asks.

"Nah," Zeke says. "I've been through plenty of things like this before. We made it to the semis of the district soccer tournament. Would have won, but the refs blew some calls."

"So it was their fault?"

"Partly. The game was dead even, then they called a penalty on us in the box. Abington got a penalty kick, and that took the steam out of us."

"So it ended 1–0?"

"Well, it actually ended up 4–0, but only because we lost all our momentum. We could've beat 'em. . . . Last spring I qualified for the tennis districts."

"You win?"

Zeke shakes his head. "I screwed up my serve and got bounced in the first round because my wrist was sore as hell."

"That's a shame," Pramod says with an obvious touch of sarcasm. "I guess you would have won it all."

"I might have. I would have at least advanced a couple of rounds."

Pramod yawns widely without covering his mouth. "Yeah, well, I guess I ought to get some sleep," he says. "I probably need to be fully awake by noon."

He's seeded second and doesn't expect to be tested until at least the semifinals.

Zeke will need to be fully awake by nine, on the other hand. None of these matches will be easy for him, but he thinks he can work his way through the bracket and upset some people. The guys he beat earlier tonight were pretty competitive.

"You'd get Buddy Malone in the semis, huh?" Zeke asks, not quite wanting to leave yet.

Pramod gives a dismissive laugh. "Malone. I'm not even *thinking* about him."

"He beat me a few weeks ago," Zeke says, shaking his head.

"Yeah, well, you aren't me." Pramod tosses his cup into the trash basket and grins. "He did beat me once. That was a year ago, at least. Not since."

"Where else did you play him?"

"I don't know. Tournaments. Be sure the door shuts behind you." Pramod strips off his shorts as he's crawling into bed.

"Okay. See you tomorrow," Zeke says.

The hallway is deserted. Zeke starts walking toward the elevator and slips his hand into his pocket again for the room key, but it isn't there. He checks his wallet, but he knows it isn't there either.

Shit. They signed release forms saying they'd be in their rooms by midnight. He can't go to the front desk for a new key.

The truth is, Zeke hadn't realized that the card thing *was* a key. He thought it was a credit card to use for room service. He also didn't realize that the door would lock automatically when he closed it.

He takes the elevator down one flight and tries his door handle, but it won't open. So he pounds on the door across the hall to get his little brother out of bed.

■ TWO ■
Beneath Her

Randy had said virtually nothing on the way over in the car that afternoon. He just sat in the back and listened to Zeke and their father go on about strategy and pressure and being remorseless to an opponent.

"These chess people, they'll fold up against an athlete like you," Mr. Mansfield said to Zeke. He cleared his throat and added—a comment Randy was certain was aimed at him—that "these thinkers are basically soft, you see. They might know the game a little better than you do, but when you turn up the heat, they'll run back to their books. You've got to *finish*, you know? Wear them down psychologically. Show them what it's like to be in the crunch zone."

Zeke just kept nodding, looking confident. Randy stared at trucks as his father sped past them on Route 81. He read the billboards for Applebee's and Scranton Toyota and Mercy Hospital. He stared at the leather upholstery on the back of the driver's seat.

"We're just as smart as any of these chess geeks," Mr. Mansfield was saying. "But our major advantage is our toughness. Nobody knocks us down; and when they do, we get up and belt 'em in the teeth."

Randy winced and checked his own front teeth with his thumb. Zeke'd given him a sharp elbow to the mouth a few days ago. Zeke was doing the dishes, and Randy bent over to toss a banana peel into the garbage can beneath the sink.

"Totally inadvertent," said Mr. Mansfield, who witnessed the whole thing. "Wise up, Randy. Don't put your head where it doesn't belong."

Randy wakes up suddenly, unsure where that pounding is coming from or even where he is. He reaches for his glasses and remembers that he's in a hotel room and one of the idiots from the tournament is trying to get him up.

He opens the door to his brother.

"What do you want?" Randy says.

"I gotta crash here. I lost my key."

Randy shakes his head but opens the door farther. "What time is it?" he asks, rubbing one eye with his finger.

"I don't even know."

Randy sighs audibly. "Were you drinking?"

"Some. What do you care?"

"I don't." Randy climbs back into bed, the one nearer the door.

Zeke flops onto the other bed and turns on the light. He frowns at the photo on the table between the beds—Randy's girlfriend, Dina.

Dina's at the house all the time, but Zeke's never even acknowledged her.

"How the hell did you lose your key?" Randy asks.

"I don't know. I guess I left it in my room."

Randy rolls over and presses the pillow against his ear. "Can you shut the light?" he says.

Zeke turns it off. "What time did you go to sleep?" he asks.

"Who knows? I watched the news at eleven. Then I was abook for a few minutes. After that."

"You were a *book*? What the hell does that mean?"

"I wasn't *a* book," Randy says. "I was reading. *Abook.* It adverb. Like aboard a train. Aloft in the air. Abook."

"That's not even a word."

"Well, it should be."

Randy loves making up words, especially since it annoys his brother.

They're quiet for several minutes. Finally, Zeke says, "I thought I won pretty easily tonight. Both matches."

"The early rounds *should* be easy," Randy says.

"Not for everybody. I mean, three-quarters of the field are already gone, so it wasn't easy for them. Everybody I played was supposedly as good as I was or better."

"Yeah," Randy says. "I forgot you didn't get seeded."

"Sure you did."

"I *did* forget."

"Believe me, getting seeded makes a *big* difference. Unseeded players are always at a disadvantage, whether they deserve to be or not."

"We still have to win the games," Randy says.

"Yeah, but you start out with an *expectation*."

"We *earned* it."

"Well, don't go getting a big head about it like these other guys," Zeke says. "Pramod thinks he's such hot shit. And Jenna or whatever her name is—the top seed—she wouldn't even play poker with us. Acted like we were all so far beneath her."

"She told me she was too sleepy to play."

"When did *you* talk to her?"

"After dinner," Randy says. "In the lobby."

"For how long?"

"I don't know. Maybe twenty minutes."

"Twenty minutes?" Zeke says. "What could you possibly have twenty minutes of stuff to talk to her about?"

"I don't know. Classic rock. She likes Dylan. The Grateful Dead. Tracy Chapman."

"Who?"

"Some singer."

After dinner, Randy had found Jenna leaning against the wall outside a room on the third floor, talking to Buddy Malone. The door was propped open with somebody's suitcase, and

Randy could see about a half dozen guys in there setting up for a poker game, including Zeke. He was hoping Zeke wouldn't be there, but it was a moot point anyway, since Randy didn't have any money to buy into the game.

"You guys playing?" Randy asked.

"Probably not," said Malone, a tall guy with frizzy red hair and a scruffy goatee. "It's already after ten and I'm beat."

Jenna wiggled her mouth and looked like she was thinking it over. "I think I'll pass," she said. "You?"

"Can't," Randy said. "No cash. No big deal, though. My brother is pretty much the last guy I'd want to get in a poker game with."

"Because he's too good?" Jenna asked.

"Because he's toxic."

Jenna laughed. "Which one is he?"

Randy peered around the door and jutted his chin toward the poker game. "That one. Dark curly hair."

"Oh." She nodded. "He's pretty cute."

Randy shrugged. "Looks are deceiving."

"You two look different."

Randy is on the pudgy side and only five foot six—which is actually a half inch taller than Zeke—with freckles and no facial hair yet. Could easily pass for a seventh grader, even though he's in ninth. He gets his dominant features from their mother; Zeke is lean and wiry and looks much more like their dad.

Malone looked at his watch and yawned. "I'll see you guys tomorrow," he said. He caught Randy's eye. "Your brother almost beat me a couple of weeks ago. But I hear you're better than he is."

"Heard right," Randy said. "*He* doesn't think so, but the record speaks for itself."

There was a lot of laughing and cursing coming from the poker game. Jenna frowned and asked Randy if he'd liked to go down to the lobby and talk.

"Sure." *All these guys her age here and she wants to hang out with me?*

They started walking down the hallway but turned back when they heard a loud crash from the poker room.

Pramod stuck his head out the door and grinned at Jenna. "A lamp broke," he said, shoving the suitcase back into the room with his foot.

"Just like that, huh?"

Pramod smirked and laughed. "Spontaneously. . . . Why aren't you in here, gorgeous?"

"Too tired," she said. "Big day tomorrow."

"This your servant?" Pramod asked, pointing at Randy. He didn't wait for an answer. "I can blow off this card game, if you're looking for a companion. If you need a massage or something."

Jenna frowned. "I don't think so. You better go clean up that lamp."

"They got it under control. I'll be in room 407 later if you change your mind. Call anytime; I'll come running."

She turned and started walking. "Don't hold your breath."

Downstairs, she took a seat on a leather couch in the lobby and folded one knee over the other. She was still wearing the beige skirt she wore to dinner; most of the others had put on jeans or sweats for the evening.

Randy had worn a black Guns n' Roses T-shirt to the

dinner, and Zeke told him he was pathetic. But it hadn't occurred to Randy to bring anything dressier.

"You into classic rock?" Jenna asked, pointing to the shirt.

"Absolutely," Randy said. "My brother hates it, so I blast it as much as possible."

"You don't like him very much, huh?"

Randy rolled his eyes and folded his arms across his chest. "He never gives me a chance to."

Randy flicks on the light, climbs out of bed, and walks over to the window. The clock says 1:56. He glances out at downtown Scranton—the gray piles of old snow around the courthouse square, the dim lights of the storefronts, the ancient Electric City neon sign atop a building across the way.

"So what else did Jenna want to know?" Zeke asks.

"What do you mean?"

"She knows she'll probably wind up playing me in the fourth round. Was she asking you about my game or something?"

"No. You never came up."

"I bet," Zeke says.

"Don't be a jerk. Like I'd give away your game to her?"

"Well, she must have had some motive for talking to you."

"Maybe she was just being friendly."

"Watch what you say if she comes up to you tomorrow."

Randy doesn't respond. He walks past the beds to the bathroom and brushes his teeth again. Dinner was garlicky and he can still taste it.

"You got any mouthwash in there?" Zeke calls.

Randy stops brushing. "Yeah," he says as toothpaste drib-
bles onto his chin.

"I didn't brush my teeth either. . . . My toothbrush is in my
room."

Randy looks into the mirror and laughs. *What an idiot,* he
thinks. He rinses his toothbrush and puts it into its blue travel
holder. He carries the toothbrush with him into the bedroom
and sets it on the table next to Dina's picture. Then he picks up
the remote and switches on the television.

Zeke gets up to gargle. "Two o'clock," he says when he
comes back. "I think *Star Trek*'s on."

"No thanks." Randy flips rapidly through the channels.

"I thought you liked that show."

"When I was *ten* maybe. Did you want to see it?"

"No. . . . I don't care."

They watch a stand-up routine for a few minutes, then
Randy turns the TV off.

"You got anything to eat?" Zeke asks.

"A bag of M&M's."

"Can I have some?"

"They're over by the window."

Zeke gets out of bed again. The candy bag is huge. He tears
it open, then picks up Randy's chessboard from the dresser. He
takes Randy's toothbrush, the phone, and the picture of Dina
off the bedside table and sets them on the shelf underneath
with the Bible. Then he pulls the table out a bit from the wall
and sets the chessboard on it.

"Want to play?" he asks.

"Sure. The pieces are in my gym bag."

"Got a better idea," Zeke says. He pours some of the

M&M's onto his sheet and separates some red ones and blue ones. "Checkers!"

He starts setting the M&M's on the board.

"What if we get kings?" Randy asks.

"If you get a king, it changes to orange; if I get one, it's brown."

Randy picks up a red M&M and holds it between his fingers. It's flattened somewhat on one side and has a lump at the edge. "Look!" he says. "A misshapen one!"

"So what?"

"Do you have any idea how rare that is?"

"No. I don't."

"It's *very* rare. Probably extremely valuable." He pops it into his mouth and chews it up.

They play two games, each winning once.

Randy brushes his teeth again, since he ate his pieces after the games.

They lie quietly again for a while.

"She's really nice, you know," Randy says.

"Who?"

"Jenna. McNulty."

"Seems kind of stuck-up to me."

"She can't help it if she's brilliant."

Zeke snorts. "She *looks* good, I'll give you that much. But she acts like she sat on a rook."

"She was pretty funny. Said Buddy Malone doesn't move his feet when he dances. Just floats his arms up and down and wiggles his hips. She demonstrated. It was hilarious."

"She went *out* with him?"

"No. She said it was at some student-leadership thing at Marywood. He kept hitting on her."

"He would. . . . Well, I would, too."

Randy doesn't respond.

"I would!" Zeke says. "What? You think I wouldn't?"

"I don't know."

"She thinks she's so frickin' gorgeous. Acts like we're all beneath her."

"You already said that already."

"So?"

"It's redundant," Randy says.

"And saying 'already *already*' isn't?"

"No, that's reinforcing. I like that."

"Well, you're a jerk," Zeke says. "And that's why she was talking to *you*. To try to make a point that she doesn't need to acknowledge any of the rest of us."

"What's that supposed to mean?"

"Nothing. . . . Like the guys her own age—guys who might actually want to go out with her like we're . . ." He hesitates over the phrase *beneath her* again and finally says, "invisible or something."

"I didn't get that impression," Randy says.

"What impression?"

"That she's a snob. I mean, imagine if *you* looked that good. Don't you think you'd get a lot of attention?"

"I don't look that good?"

"You know what I mean."

"I think I look good," Zeke says. "I'm in *shape*, at least."

"So?"

"And I don't have a frickin' Cub Scout haircut like you do."

"What the hell's a Cub Scout haircut?"

"And you're wearing *pajamas*, like you're seven years old."

"What does that have to do with anything?" Randy asks.

"Just shut up and go to sleep."

"I've tried that. You keep butting in."

"Yeah, well, don't go getting ideas that she's interested in *you*, for God's sake," Zeke says. "Just because she talks to you about music. She was probably trying to find out about me. About my game, at least."

"Like I said, you never came up."

"Then just shut up and go to sleep. It's like three o'clock in the morning. We've got a tournament in a couple of hours."

"You think I don't know that?" Randy rolls to his side, facing away from Zeke's bed, and tries to lie still. After about thirty seconds, he throws the sheet off his body, says, "It's hotter than hell in here," and yanks off his socks, tossing them one at a time over Zeke's head against the window.

"What was that?" Zeke asks.

"My socks."

Zeke starts laughing. "You know where *my* socks are?"

"No. How would I?"

"I don't know either. I took off my shoes and socks during the poker game and left them in the room."

Randy starts laughing, too. "So you're totally de-shoed?"

"Completely."

"Whose room was it?"

"I don't even know. Some kid from North Pocono, I think."

"So you lost your key, your socks, *and* your shoes?"

"Yeah. You got some I can borrow for tomorrow?"

"You could wear my sandals."

"Thanks."

"You win any money?" Randy asks.

"Nah. I lost about two bucks."

"Who won?"

"Pramod. I think he was cheating. He kept getting aces."

"Were they his cards?"

"Yeah."

"He probably had them marked."

"Probably. He couldn't have won more than fifteen bucks, though. If that."

Randy looks at the clock again. It's 3:17.

"We tried to find her room," Zeke says.

"What for?"

"I don't know. To hassle her, I guess. Try to shake her up a little; mess with her head for tomorrow."

"I don't think she's easily perturbulated," Randy says.

"We would have found a way."

"Real mature."

"Hey, that's competition," Zeke says. "You have to get in your opponent's head somehow. Psych them out."

"So I hear. But it probably would have just psyched her *up*."

"Well, anyway, it would have cost her some rest time. She's probably been asleep for five hours."

"Unlike us," Randy says with a sigh.

19

"Yeah, we're toast if we don't get to sleep soon."

"So shut up, why don't ya?"

"You shut up, too."

"I will when you do."

"Consider it done."

■ THREE ■
Fried Eggs Hard

It seems like they've only been asleep for five minutes when there's another knock, but Randy looks at the clock and it's nearly 7:30.

His brother rolls off the bed and their father's at the door, having driven the thirty miles from Sturbridge this morning. He looks a lot like Zeke—short and lean with thick, curly hair—but he's wearing a sports jacket and a green golf shirt over new jeans and loafers. He smells of cologne. His speech has an odd diction from growing up in North Jersey: the word *just* comes out almost as *junst,* for example; *milk* spills over toward *melk.*

"I figured you might be over here," he says to Zeke, "since you weren't in your room." He frowns when he notices that

Randy's still in bed. "Better move your butt, Randy. You should have been up an hour ago."

Randy props up on one elbow and wipes his nose with the other hand.

"What for?"

"The thing starts at *nine*," Mr. Mansfield says.

"It's *downstairs*."

"You need to eat and get psyched up."

"It's *chess*, Dad. Not a football game."

Mr. Mansfield rolls his eyes and looks at Zeke. "Like he'd know," he says quietly.

Zeke smirks and mumbles, "Lard butt," which Randy hears from him about thirty times a day.

Screw you both, Randy thinks. He *is* a little soft, maybe fifteen pounds heavier than he ought to be. *But I don't spend every minute worrying about my speed or my moves or my physique like Zeke does; like Dad thinks I should, too.*

And Dad calls him *Ace*. Everybody else calls him Zeke, which, after all, is his name. Randy refers to him as Ass.

"Don't squander this opportunity, Randy," Mr. Mansfield says. "Show some *gumption* for once. You can kick these people's tails if you set your mind to it."

"It's *chess*, Dad," Randy says again. "No kicking allowed."

"Well, you can metaphorically kick their butts, you know."

"Yeah, or I could systematically outmaneuver them without making believe it's a professional wrestling match."

Zeke jumps in. "Some of these guys are vicious," he says pointedly. "Dad's right, they'll intimidate the hell out of you if you don't show some attitude of your own."

"Half of the *guys* are girls," Randy says.

"They'll still whip your lazy ass."

"Get out of bed, Randy," Mr. Mansfield says. He points straight down at the floor. "I've already got us a table for breakfast. Be down there in ten minutes. This is *important*. I shouldn't have to remind you of that."

"I know what it is," Randy says. He sits up and looks at his bare feet.

"What are you wearing?" his father asks.

"Now?"

"For the *tournament*."

"What difference does it make?"

"You want to look sharp. Awe these people a little. Let them know you mean business."

"I didn't bring a suit, if that's what you mean."

"What *did* you bring?"

"My regular clothes. I don't know; I think I've got a clean T-shirt in my bag."

"At least tuck it in." Mr. Mansfield puts his hand on the doorknob. "Ten minutes." Then he leaves.

Randy stands up and looks at Zeke. "Maybe I should put on war paint."

"Where are those sandals?" Zeke asks. "I'm gonna go down to the desk to get another key to my room."

"In my bag." Randy walks over to the window and picks up his socks. He opens his bag and tosses the sandals, one at a time, toward his brother. Then he picks up the package of M&M's. "Might as well eat some of these before I brush my teeth," he says. "You want any?"

"Sure."

"We finished the blue ones."

"They all taste the same anyway," Zeke says.

"Not exactly."

"Yes they do. You think blue dye tastes different than orange?"

"How could it not?"

"It's *food* coloring," Zeke says. "It has no taste of its own. It's just sugar over chocolate."

Randy pours a couple of dozen M&M's onto his bed. "Then let's do a little test."

"Dad's waiting for us."

"Yeah. To eat *breakfast*. That's what we're doing."

Randy separates the candies into four small piles: red, orange, green, and brown. The yellow ones go back into the bag. *Can't have too many variables*, he thinks. He picks up a red one and holds it between his thumb and first finger. He looks it over good, pops it into his mouth, then nods at Zeke.

"Red," Randy says.

"Amazing."

"That wasn't a guess. I'm just getting the flavor of each straight in my head." He picks up a green one, holds it in his mouth for a few seconds with his eyes shut, then chews and swallows. "Now the brown."

And then the orange.

"Okay," Randy says. "Now I'll shut my eyes, and you feed them to me at random and I'll identify them by their various and subtle taste differences."

"Sure you will."

"Try me."

Zeke rolls his eyes and shakes his head. "Dad's gonna kill us."

"This'll take five seconds." Randy sits on the bed with his eyes closed and his mouth open.

"I'm *not* putting these in your mouth."

"Then just hand them to me one at a time. You can blindfold me if you want."

"Just keep your eyes shut."

Zeke frowns over the piles, then picks up a brown one and hands it to Randy.

"Brown," Randy says almost immediately.

"You looked."

"I swear I didn't."

The next one is orange, but Randy says red.

"Wrong," Zeke says with a sneer.

"What was it?"

"Orange."

"They're nearly identical. Very close. I knew it wasn't green or brown."

"Sure you did."

Zeke tries to trip him up by handing him another orange one. But Randy gets it right.

He misses the next one, guessing red when it's actually green. Then the phone rings.

"Two out of four," Zeke says.

"Two and a half," Randy says. "That's pretty good."

The phone rings again, and Randy picks it up.

"Where the hell are you guys?" Mr. Mansfield asks.

"We're just leaving. Zeke was screwing around."

Randy starts scooping up the M&M's and putting them back in the bag. "Are we supposed to check out now?" he asks.

"They said we can keep the rooms until we're eliminated. So we can come back up if there's time between the rounds."

"One more." Randy spreads his arms and mouth wide and closes his eyes.

Zeke picks up another brown one and Randy gets it right.

"Okay, so maybe the brown ones have a distinct taste," Zeke says. "All chocolate. But you didn't convince me on the other ones."

"I think I did pretty good."

"Well, you're an idiot."

Randy pulls on an oversized Allman Brothers T-shirt and his sneakers. They walk toward the elevator, and Randy pushes the arrow to go down.

But Zeke starts walking again, heading for the stairs at the end of the hall. "Tell Dad I'll be there in two minutes," he says. "He's probably camped out by the elevator to give us more advice."

Randy nods.

"And don't you say one frickin' word about me getting locked out last night," Zeke says, walking backward now. "You are *dead meat* if he hears about that. You got it?"

"Just shut up."

"He'd blame Mom."

"How could he blame *her?*"

"He always blames her when we screw up."

When the elevator opens, Jenna McNulty is standing inside. She looks as if she's going to a job interview—dark linen suit, modest makeup, carrying a briefcase. The briefcase has a small decal that says Scranton Prep.

"Morning," Randy says as he steps in.

"Hi," she says cheerfully. "Sleep well?"

"I don't remember." Randy gives a sly smile. "My stupid brother had me up all night."

"Just as well. I was so nervous I barely slept a wink."

"You're the top seed. You should be completely counter-nervoused."

"Yeah, but there's a lot of pressure."

"You'll do great."

"You, too."

They reach the ground floor, and Jenna walks briskly toward the conference room where the tournament will be, her heels clicking on the lobby floor. Randy strolls toward the coffee shop to meet his father. He notices Zeke waiting in a short line by the front desk.

Mr. Mansfield is drumming his fingers on the table as Randy walks in. The boys' mother is working on this Saturday morning (she's a cashier at Wal-Mart; Mr. Mansfield is a loan officer at the Sturbridge National Bank), but she'll drive over this afternoon with Dina if Randy makes the semifinals.

"Where's Ace?" Mr. Mansfield asks.

"*Ace* is looking for his toothbrush."

Mr. Mansfield checks his watch. "You better order. I already ate."

"Shouldn't I wait for Zeke?"

"Zeke can take care of himself. You order." The plate in front of Mr. Mansfield has a gooey yellow residue from eggs and the crust from a slice of rye toast. He's drinking coffee. He waves his hand at a waitress.

"Hi," Randy says as she comes over. "I'll have two fried eggs *hard,* not runny at all, some ham and . . . You have fruit?"

"Cantaloupe."

"That and orange juice."

"Would you like toast or home fries?"

"White toast. Yeah, fries, too."

Mr. Mansfield puts a fist decisively on the table. "Do you have a strategy for this morning?"

Randy shrugs. "I don't even know who I play yet."

"Whom."

"Say what?"

"You don't know *whom* you play."

Randy just rolls his eyes.

"See, that's why you needed to snap to it this morning. They've got the brackets posted outside the conference room."

"I'll look at it after I eat."

"You play some unseeded kid named Brian Burke. From Holy Cross. What do you know about him?"

"Everything you just told me."

"What?"

"I never heard of him."

"He's in the final sixteen and you never heard of him? I'll tell you what, I guarantee he knows all about *you*."

"So?"

"So you need to prepare yourself, Randy." Mr. Mansfield picks up his coffee cup and looks into it. He scans the restaurant, then sets the cup down and puts the crust of toast into his mouth, chewing as he talks. "Anyway, after you beat him, you get—hold on." He reaches into his pocket and takes out a napkin. "I wrote it down. Either Lucy Ahada from Dunmore—she's seeded right ahead of you in fourth—or Ethan Rosenfeld from Midvale. You know them?"

28

"Lucy beat me in a dual match a few weeks ago, but I figured her out. I can probably win. The guy from Midvale won't beat her. Not a chance."

"What's her game like? This Lucy Ahada?"

"Deliberate. Patient. She loves her knights."

"Why'd she beat you?"

"Because she's good."

"Was it close?"

"Very."

Mr. Mansfield stares at Randy, not blinking, narrowing his eyes and looking cold.

Randy glances away. When he looks back, his dad is still staring.

"What?" Randy asks.

Mr. Mansfield raises a finger and points to his right eye.

"What?" Randy says again, losing patience.

Mr. Mansfield gives a smirky half smile. "That's called intimidation," he says, leaning back in his chair. "It's our best weapon, pal." He drops his voice and leans forward again. "Especially against a girl. You're *all* business out there, you hear me? Put on the game face and she'll fold up."

Randy bites down on his lip to keep from laughing. The waitress delivers his food, and Mr. Mansfield asks her for a fresh cup of coffee.

Randy's nearly done with his meal when Zeke finally arrives. He's wearing an unbuttoned long-sleeved white shirt over a fresh T-shirt. Also Randy's sandals and no socks.

"Success?" Randy asks.

Zeke looks away from Randy but says, "Yep."

"You check the brackets?" Mr. Mansfield asks.

29

"Not yet," Zeke says.

"You've got the eighth seed. Some kid from Hazleton. Phan something. Donald. Or Dennis."

"Derek Pham."

"Okay, so you know him. See, Randy? He's up on this stuff. He knows who's who."

"Whom's whom."

"What?"

"I said, 'Very impressive.'" Randy shoves a large chunk of ham into his mouth, grabs his second piece of toast, and stands. "I'm going to my room to get cleaned up."

"Be down here *no later* than eight-thirty-five."

Randy salutes and walks away. When he turns back, Mr. Mansfield and Zeke are trying to stare each other down, working on Zeke's intimidation face.

It's been more than two months since that play-off game, but Zeke can bring back every feeling, every emotion, within seconds. Almost inconceivably, they were outplaying the top-ranked team in the area, dominating the game even though neither side had scored yet.

Zeke had the ball, well past midfield, with an open sideline before him and a couple of teammates running parallel. The angle was just right; he feinted once, then streaked past an Abington defender and sprinted into the clear. In a few more strides, he'd loft that ball toward the front of the goal.

He can still feel his foot meeting the ball, sending a perfect pass toward Greg Foley, a can't-miss opportunity to score. Zeke felt a surge of adrenaline; he'd placed the ball just right.

Somehow Greg fell down. A dry field, a wide-open space by the goal, but Greg was eating turf. The goalie booted the ball long and hard, and suddenly it was Abington with the numbers, with an onslaught of players near the Sturbridge goal as Zeke and Greg and the other forwards raced frantically back.

Players went down, the ball flew off the field, and a red card went up. The penalty shot rippled the net. Zeke punched at the air and cursed.

By halftime it was 3–0.

He remembers walking off the field, right past his father, who was already complaining to the officials. "You were the best one out there," Mr. Mansfield said, catching up.

Zeke scowled, but he nodded. *Whatever you say, Dad,* he thought. But even then, he knew it wasn't true.

Randy had come down from the bleachers and was walking cautiously toward his brother. Zeke looked up. "Don't say one frickin' word," he said sharply. He jabbed a finger in Randy's direction. "At least I was out there. At least I had the balls to try."

It's 8:21 when Randy enters his room. He clicks on the TV and finds a fishing show on ESPN. The TVs in the players' rooms are blocked from tuning in the pay-per-view movies. Randy tried last night anyway.

He takes one each of a black rook, bishop, pawn, knight, and the king and places them in predetermined positions on his chessboard, then does the same with a white bishop, rook, two pawns, and the king.

He stares at the board for several seconds, then shifts the black rook three spaces forward. He smiles slightly and tips the white king onto its side.

Last night was the first in his life that he ever spent alone, at least until Zeke showed up. He watched a college basketball game on TV, took a hot thirty-six-minute shower, and read the room-service menu and the description of the hotel's amenities.

Randy has his own bedroom at home, but there's never been a night when at least one of his parents wasn't under the same roof. Lately he's started to wonder when the time will come that his parents are always under different roofs.

He enters the bathroom, brushes his teeth, and picks up the small containers of shampoo, conditioner, and skin cream and drops them into his gym bag.

He looks at himself in the mirror above the sink. His short, straight brown hair is parted on one side, and his ears stick out slightly. He turns on the hot-water faucet and dampens his fingers, then runs them through his hair, pushing it back off his forehead and having it fall a bit more symmetrically to each side.

He tucks in his T-shirt and grabs a long-sleeved brown corduroy shirt from his bag and puts it on, buttoning it up and nodding at himself in the mirror.

He checks the clock: 8:33. So he looks around the room, picks up the key from the dresser, and heads downstairs.

Pramod Eskederian and Buddy Malone are in the elevator. Malone is wearing a sleeveless black workout shirt, and his right bicep is encircled by a tattoo that looks like a chain. He's won district swimming championships in the butterfly and backstroke, and he's already been accepted at MIT.

"Hey, little Mansfield," Buddy says. They've never met in a match. Buddy defeated Zeke in the season opener back in November, when Zeke still had the first chair for Sturbridge.

"Your brother up yet?" asks Pramod, who's wearing a gray V-necked sweater that says HARVARD in small red letters.

"Yeah."

"He's probably hungover. We got pretty wasted last night."

"You did, huh?"

"Yeah. He didn't get back to his own room until four."

Randy shrugs. "Heard you bepokered well."

"What?"

"I heard you won some poker money."

"A little," Pramod says. "Maybe two hundred bucks. I didn't play very long. Met a few ladies and"—he breaks into a big grin—"showed them my best moves."

The elevator doors open at the lobby. "Good luck, guys," Randy says.

"As if we need it," Pramod replies.

Randy stops and glances at the brackets.

THIRD ROUND. 9:00 a.m. SATURDAY

A. Jenna McNulty (Scranton Prep) (no. 1 seed) vs. Darius Haywood (Stroudsburg)

B. Derek Pham (Hazleton) (8) vs. Zeke Mansfield (Sturbridge)

C. Lucy Ahada (Dunmore) (4) vs. Ethan Rosenfeld (Midvale)

33

D. Randy Mansfield (Sturbridge) (5) vs. Brian Burke (Holy Cross)

E. Pramod Eskederian (Wilkes-Barre Jesuit) (2) vs. Tami Nixon (Scranton)

F. Silvio Vega (Meyers) vs. Garion Liberti (North Pocono)

G. Buddy Malone (Weston South) (3) vs. Stephanie Irving (Tunkhannock)

H. Colin Lucas (Abington Heights) vs. Serena Leung (East Scranton)

QUARTERFINALS, APPROXIMATELY 10:15 a.m.

I. Match A winner vs. Match B winner

J. C winner vs. D winner

K. E winner vs. F winner

L. G winner vs. H winner

SEMIFINALS, 1:00 p.m.

I winner vs. J winner

K winner vs. L winner

CHAMPIONSHIP, APPROXIMATELY 2:15 p.m.

Randy enters the conference room. He takes a glazed doughnut off a tray and eats it, then looks around for a napkin. He finds a stack of them, but his fingers still feel sticky. So he goes back to the lobby and enters the bathroom to wash his hands.

A toilet flushes and an energetic kid with very short hair and slightly crossed eyes pops out of the stall. He's wearing a letterman's jacket that says Holy Cross Baseball. "How's it going?" he asks, vigorously washing his hands at the sink next to Randy's.

"I'm all right. Are you Brian Burke?"

"Yeah."

"I'm Randy Mansfield. I think we play first thing."

Burke sticks out a wet hand and Randy shakes it. Burke's grip is strong, and he has big shoulders. "You stay here last night?" he asks.

Randy nods.

"I went home after the matches. Just got back about five minutes ago. What'd I miss?"

"Nothing much. Some of them played cards."

"Figured I'd sleep better in my own bed," Burke says. "We only live about ten minutes away." He runs his hand over his chin, peering into the mirror and checking a few small zits. He pushes the door open with his shoulder and says, "See you out there."

And for the first time all weekend, Randy begins to feel nervous. He takes a deep inhale, but his heart is pounding and his stomach feels cold. He can taste those fried eggs.

The clock in the lobby says 8:54. He walks back to the conference room and looks at the brackets again.

Eskederian and Malone are over by one of the windows, laughing. Jenna McNulty is seated at the table where her first match will be, chin in one hand, staring at the floor. Zeke is leaning against the wall, hands in his pockets, glancing around. Brian Burke is doing *push-ups* over in the corner.

Randy looks for his father, but he isn't in the room. Randy is beyond nervous now; he's scared.

The tournament's Regional Director—Dr. Thomas Kerrigan— is at the registration table, checking his bracket sheet. He's a somewhat dour man who teaches in the Classics Department at the University of Scranton, which is directly across the street from the hotel. He looks at his wristwatch, says something to his assistant, and asks the players to take their seats for the next round.

■ FOUR ■
Fourth-and-Goal

Zeke walks as casually as he can toward the table at the back of
the room, where Derek Pham is waiting. He avoids eye contact
with Randy. He's seen the brackets; he knows they could be
facing each other this afternoon.

As hard as Zeke works in sports, as much limited success
as he's had, there's that realization bubbling just beneath the
surface that Randy would be a better athlete than Zeke if he
wanted to be. Randy'd been such a good soccer player when
he was little, dominating games as a first grader against other
kids from town in the YMCA league on the narrow field next
to the river. He had agility and a natural touch on the ball,
plus a good sense of the game. He seemed to love every second
of it—the practices, the pregame warm-ups, the "Go-oooooo

Falcons!" cheers. The coach, who was the mother of one of the girls on the team, laughed all the time and didn't try very hard to impart any strategy.

When January came, the soccer program resumed on the Y's creaky indoor basketball court, with fewer players per side and those soft, cloth-covered balls that don't bounce much on the wood. Mr. Mansfield volunteered to coach, so of course Randy ended up on his dad's team, the Panthers. Zeke, a fourth grader and a fine player already, was drafted to help as a junior assistant.

The team developed into an aggressive, good-passing unit that easily won every game and rarely gave up a goal. Randy ended up in tears after two of the games, but he kept playing for a few more seasons before deciding soccer wasn't for him.

As for Zeke, except for that assistant-coaching stint, he's never had a chance to be the big brother in the equation. Randy was always the better student, always had more friends. He also found that first girlfriend, and he usually whips Zeke's butt in chess.

It's clear to Zeke that their father has pretty much written Randy off as an athlete, but this chess thing might be a decent consolation. They never hear the end of how Mr. Mansfield was a year-round athlete back in high school, playing on the kickoff and punt teams in football, getting some decent time on the JV basketball squad before being cut as a senior, and earning a letter in baseball despite spending most of the season recording stats from the bench. He never won a championship or anything, but always said he could have if he'd been given a fair shot at it. And he was sure he could have made the baseball team at Bergen Community College but passed up the chance to walk on because of his blistering academic load.

So he was only too happy to impart all he'd learned to his sons. That's why he'd have Zeke up at the high school tennis courts in fourteen-degree weather endlessly practicing his serve. He told Zeke that he saw everything that he'd been in his older son, and he wasn't about to let circumstances screw this kid out of his well-deserved stardom.

Randy glances nervously at his father, who's sitting in a row of folding chairs at one end of the room. The parents and other spectators are not allowed to speak to the players during the games; any coaching would be grounds for disqualification. So Randy swallows hard and takes his seat across from Brian Burke.

Burke has his sleeves rolled up. His slightly crossed eyes are fixed on the board.

Randy has the white pieces, so he'll move first. The clock is to his right; it's a simple device with buttons on top to start and stop the timer as each player makes a move. Each player in this tournament has thirty minutes per game; his or her time begins as soon as the opponent hits the clock.

Randy didn't use even a third of his time in either game last night. He takes a deep breath, starts the clock, moves a pawn two spaces forward to d4, and smacks the button to shift the time over to Burke.

Burke looks surprised, as if Randy's extremely basic opening move was something original and daring. He hesitates with one hand over his queenside knight, then blinks slowly and puts the hand to his mouth.

After nearly a minute, Burke makes a move that mirrors Randy's, shifting a pawn to d5 and sitting back with his arms folded across his chest.

Randy holds back a smile. *This guy won two games last night?* He immediately brings out his queenside bishop and looks up to try to meet Burke's eyes. But Burke is squinting intently at the board. And again he makes an identical move with his own bishop.

Randy guesses this is how Burke always plays when he has black, mirroring his opponent for a series of moves before establishing himself. But he senses that Burke is waiting for him to make an error rather than going on the attack.

Randy develops his queenside knight, moves a second pawn, and soon castles on that same side. He's already in a position of strength, controlling the center of the board. Burke is tapping a finger loudly on the table. Jenna McNulty, at an adjacent table, shoots him an icy look and he stops.

Burke is taking a long time with his next move, and Randy's eyes drift over to Jenna's board. He recognizes her strategy right away, an adventurous opening known as the Sicilian Dragon. It's the same game Zeke usually plays, so Randy's become proficient at dismantling it.

Burke makes an ill-advised move, and Randy swiftly captures his queen with a knight. Burke retaliates by taking the knight with a pawn, but the exchange of pieces is greatly in Randy's favor. He wipes out that same pawn with his bishop, and Burke's frown grows deeper.

Ten minutes, Randy thinks, calculating how long it'll be

before he wins the game. Astonishingly, Pramod is already on his feet a few tables away, shaking hands with his opponent and smirking. Randy watches him leave the room, then looks back at his own board.

"Check," Burke says, gesturing with a finger toward his bishop, which is attacking Randy's king.

Randy purses his lips and ponders whether to take the bishop with his rook or his queen. He decides on the rook. Burke lets out a sigh and slumps a bit in his seat.

Randy's material advantage grows quickly, and it becomes obvious that Burke is playing for a draw. The early loss of his queen is fatal, though, and Randy forces checkmate a few minutes later.

All of the other games are still in progress. Randy heads for the door, and his father follows him out.

"Was he any good?" Mr. Mansfield asks.

Randy shrugs. "He made some absurdly bad moves."

"Probably choked."

"Seemed like it."

"Could you tell how your brother was doing?"

Randy shakes his head. "He was on the totally other side, practically de-roomed from me."

"I'm sure he's doing fine. . . . We had a little pep talk before he went in."

Burke comes out of the room in his letterman's jacket and walks past, shaking his head slowly. "Nice game," he says.

"You, too."

Burke laughs. "I sucked. Don't know where my head was at."

"There's a lot of pressure," Randy says. "It's easy to mess up."

"Yeah, well, good luck the rest of the way. I'm out of here."

"Don't feel too bad," Mr. Mansfield says. "You probably lost to the champion."

"Dad."

"What?"

"Don't get carried away. There's some ass-kicking players in there."

"Be one of them."

"Easy to say."

Malone exits the room, followed a few seconds later by Jenna McNulty. Both are smiling.

"Let's go in," Mr. Mansfield says. "See what your brother is up to."

Zeke is frowning deeply—nearly a scowl—and is staring at his black king, which is the only piece he has left. Derek Pham has just a queen to go with his king, but he's forcing Zeke toward the corner of the board and his victory seems inevitable.

An Asian couple is standing as close to the table as they're permitted, about twenty feet away, and beaming with pride. Pham himself is showing no emotion, but he quickly moves his queen and sits back.

Zeke lets out a snorty laugh, gives Pham a hard look, and says, "Stalemate." He stands up and takes a few steps away while Pham stares openmouthed at the board. Zeke is not in check, but he has no legal moves that would not *put* him in check. So the game is a draw.

Zeke makes a big show of sitting back down and sweeping the white pieces over to his side. "Need a break?" he asks somewhat pointedly.

Pham shakes his head and sets up the black pieces. And they start over.

Zeke moves rapidly now, keeping a sharp gaze on Pham between moves. Pham is clearly flustered from his stumble in the previous game, and Zeke takes control of the center of the board. He wins easily, smacks his right fist loudly into his left palm, and reaches across to shake Pham's hand.

Zeke's is the last game to finish, and the remaining players are milling around in the lobby, waiting to begin the quarter-finals. He's permitted a twenty-minute break, even if the other games begin on time.

The new matchups are quickly posted:

McNulty vs. Z. Mansfield
Ahada vs. R. Mansfield
Eskederian vs. Vega
Malone vs. Leung

Pham looks totally dejected, and Mr. Mansfield goes over to talk to him and his parents. Randy walks over to Zeke.

"I gotta get a drink," Zeke says. So they go out to the lobby and put a handful of quarters into the machine. Randy gets a Sprite.

"I clobbered him," Zeke says, taking a swig of Coke.

"You nailed him pretty good. My guy was weak. No idea how he got this far."

"People get intimidated. Pressure, you know."

"Speaking of. You get Jenna next."

Zeke shrugs. "I'm up for it."

"You ever watch her play?"

"You mean, study her game?"

"Yeah."

"Nope."

Randy looks around, then leans in a little. "You can beat her, believe me. Let her have her first three or four moves; you'll see what's coming."

"How do you know?"

"She was right next to me this morning. Burke was so weak I had a chance to watch some of her game."

"Oh."

"Just play your game, but be very aware of what she does."

"What are you trying to tell me?"

"Just be aware."

Zeke turns away, scratching his jaw. "Like I need your help."

Pramod walks over with his too-confident smile. He stands next to Zeke and says, "Pulled one out of your ass, huh?"

"He got lucky in the first game," Zeke says, taking a half step back. Pramod always stands too close. "I showed him who's boss in the second."

"Pham sucks anyway. I beat him in about two minutes a couple of weeks ago."

"Big deal."

Pramod studies the fingernails of his right hand. "You get the princess next."

"Who?" Zeke asks. *Don't let this jerk get to you again.*

"You know who."

"I ain't worried." Zeke closes one eye, holds his Coke can up to his face, and looks into it with his open eye.

44

"See if you can at least make her sweat a little. Drain her concentration so she won't be too pumped when I play her in the final."

Randy butts in. "You scared of her or something?"

Pramod lets out a dismissive sound, blowing his breath out through his teeth. "Not a chance."

"She has to get past me first," Zeke says.

"Right," says Pramod. "I'm sure she's insanely worried."

Randy locks his eyes on Pramod's and juts his head toward the conference room. "Why don't you go find yourself some more 'ladies'?"

"In there?"

"Anywhere."

"You think I can't?"

Randy laughs. "You're such a bullshitter. Two hundred bucks, huh?"

Pramod glares at Zeke. "Something like that," he says.

"Anyway," Randy says, "this is a private conversation." He raises his hand and wiggles his fingers. "Bye-bye, Pramod."

"Screw you." But he walks away.

"What a putz," Randy says.

Zeke is embarrassed. He should have been the one to tell Pramod to screw off, not his little brother. "He's totally full of himself," he says.

"As if we aren't?"

"Not like that guy," Zeke says.

"As I was saying, you can beat her."

"Like *I* was saying, I don't need your help." Zeke looks up at the clock and says, "I'm going upstairs for a minute." He walks toward the elevator.

■ ■ ■

Randy plunks himself onto the leather couch and looks at a spiky plant in a pot. Zeke has always been like that, resistant to any outreach from his brother. On the scale in Randy's head, guys like Pramod are near the upper echelon of jerks, with Zeke a notch or two below but well up there nonetheless. A guy like Buddy Malone—smart and talented and successful—somehow manages to hardly be a jerk at all, at least to Randy.

The leather cushions hiss as Mr. Mansfield sits down. "Concentrating on your next match?" he asks.

"Yeah."

The truth is, Randy hasn't even thought about it. Lucy Ahada is small and quiet, but she seemed very nice when she beat him a few weeks ago. As usual, he'll see how the match develops rather than going in with a definitive strategy.

"Remember," his father says, "you start out with an advantage."

"How so?"

Mr. Mansfield lowers his voice. "You're a *man*."

"Oh yeah." Randy says it slowly, with mock surprise in his voice. "I'm very bemasculant. I forgot."

"Don't *ever* forget that."

"Right. I suppose that'll help Zeke a *lot* against Jenna."

"Listen, Jenna hasn't won anything that matters, okay? Dual matches and some half-assed tournaments. This one is *big*. Your brother is game-tested. On the *field*. We'll see how the chess queen holds up against that kind of pressure."

"This isn't soccer."

Mr. Mansfield leans forward and pokes a thumb into Randy's

46

arm. "You don't get it, do you? I don't care if it's chess or soccer or business negotiations. When you've taken a few hits"—he jabs the thumb harder—"been under the boards with an elbow in your chest or it's fourth-and-goal and your mouth is bleeding, *that's* when you learn about toughness. That's when you find out if you've got what it takes to kick anybody's rear end. Whatever the situation. You hear me?"

Randy shuts his eyes, opens them in a hurry, and nods. "Loud and clear," he says, rubbing his arm where his father jabbed it.

"Yeah, you have to be smart," Mr. Mansfield says. "Yeah, you have to know chess. You have to be constantly aware." He makes a circle with his thumb and first finger and pushes it hard into the air. "But everything else being equal, it's the one who makes the other one crack that'll win. The one who gets in his opponent's head and stays there."

■ FIVE ■
Unslept-in

Zeke brushes his teeth for the third time this morning and stares at himself in the mirror. He's got *two* opponents in his head; how good can that be? Jenna has coolly disposed of her first three opponents and hasn't lost to anyone younger than forty for at least six months. And Pramod—hell, Zeke would have to win twice more just to face Pramod—he's got Zeke rattled as well.

They both think they're such hot shit.

And Zeke lets Pramod do that to him, insult him to his face and get away with it.

Frickin' Randy stands up and tells Pramod to get lost; how bullshit is that? Because Randy's such a dweeb he doesn't even know what's going on. Thinks he can chat up Jenna McNulty. Like she wasn't laughing at him in her head? Like Pramod wasn't thinking what an annoying little piece of shit Randy is?

He spits out the toothpaste and cups some water into his mouth.

Randy's trying to give me advice about how to beat Jenna? Might as well try to give me advice about sports or girlfriends. Like I'd listen. Like he could tell me anything I don't already know.

Zeke scowls into the mirror, then wipes his face with a towel. He hangs the towel over the shower-curtain rod, then leaves the bathroom. He pulls the bedspread down on his unslept-in bed, pulls off the sandals, and climbs under the sheets. He kicks his legs around, pushes both pillows to one side, and gets out, leaving the sheets and the blankets in a heap.

He puts the sandals back on—*Randy's stupid sandals*—and lies back on the bed, staring at the ceiling.

There was a girl back in ninth grade. Luanne. A bunch of them played basketball one night that May, on the outside court off Church Street. Mostly guys. They were hanging around after, drinking Gatorade, and she said, "Let's go over to the park." Zeke was supposed to be home already, but she talked him into it. They made out for about six minutes on a bench. She moved away that summer, but it counted.

He sits up quickly and looks at the clock. *Shit. Late.*

He bolts out the door and runs down the stairs, leaving his room key on the dresser again. The other three matches are under way when he enters the conference room, and everyone looks up at him.

The Regional Director clears his throat and motions Zeke over. "Everything all right?" he whispers.

"Yeah. Had a stomachache."

"Feeling better now?"

"Yeah. I'm fine."

They've reconfigured the tables. All four games are well within sight of the spectators now. Jenna has her side of the board set up and is sitting with her legs crossed.

Zeke glances at the three games in progress. Buddy Malone has his hands against the table, leaning back and balancing his chair on its two back legs. It appears to be his move, the way he's fixated on the board. His opponent, Serena Leung, has a confident smile, as if she's just made a significant move. She's dressed in black jeans and a black polo shirt, with untied white sneakers and splayed-out feet. Her short hair is gelled, and there's a small silver cross on a chain around her neck. All day long she's been applying ChapStick between moves.

Pramod seems to be making short work of Silvio Vega, managing to look both bored and amused as he waits for Vega to move.

Randy and Ahada are deep in concentration, both looking exceptionally young and out of place among the other quarter-finalists.

The Regional Director looks at his watch and whispers to Zeke, "You can have four more minutes if you need."

Zeke nods. "I'll be right back," he says.

He heads straight for the bathroom. He really does have a stomachache now. Nerves and breakfast sausage.

Zeke asked a girl to the junior prom last spring. Waited too long, though. It seemed like a sure thing back in February, when they spent a lot of time joking around and talking about sports in study hall. He figured he could put off asking her until March. By mid-April he finally got up the courage, even though they hadn't really said much to each other in weeks. She was sweet about it, but she'd already accepted another offer.

Zeke finally takes his seat across from Jenna. Pramod's game seems to be nearing completion, but the other two matches look like they could go either way.

Jenna smiles and offers her hand. "Good luck," she says.

"You, too." Zeke does not smile back. He sets up the black pieces and chews on the side of his lip. He's been waiting to hear from the state colleges at Kutztown and Bloomsburg. Jenna's been offered a full ride to Princeton. The odds of him beating her are minuscule.

He turns his head toward his father and gets a thumbs-up in return.

All those practice serves, Zeke's thinking, *all those push-ups and wind sprints*. They're not a lot of help right now. Worth about as much as a misshapen M&M. "You have any idea how rare that is?" someone once asked him. "Very rare."

But sometimes very rare things happen.

■ SIX ■
Nobody Dances Well

Randy keeps track of his brother's game as best he can, ascertaining that Jenna's using the same opening as before. He tries to catch Zeke's eye to make sure he's caught on, but Zeke wouldn't acknowledge Randy for a million dollars. So Randy shifts his focus back to his own match, which he senses is moving in the right direction for him.

Lucy Ahada reminds him a lot of his girlfriend, Dina—slight build, airy demeanor, ambiguous ethnic background—so he automatically feels a sense of affection for her. She studies the board for several seconds before every move but never hesitates once she's decided what to do. She catches Randy's eye, then looks at the board again until he's responded.

She always gives a slight, polite smile after Randy's move but never betrays concern or pleasure.

She hasn't altered her strategy much from the narrow defeat she handed Randy in last month's dual match. So while she pays perhaps too much attention to bringing out her knights, Randy puts two pawns in position to limit the knights' effectiveness in the center of the board.

Dina went through the Catholic grade school, so Randy hadn't known her until they started high school and he sat behind her in American history. She was always turning around and rolling her eyes when the obnoxious teacher said something particularly annoying, and she seemed to enjoy Randy's made-up words. And Randy sometimes did childish things like fastening paper clips to Dina's collar or flicking tiny wads of paper onto her desk. He heard through another girl in the class that Dina wanted him to ask her out. But he was very passive about things like that. Scared, in fact.

So Dina waited until mid-October, then turned around one afternoon and said, "There's a dance after the homecoming football game on Friday."

"So?"

"You planning to go?"

"No."

"Well, make plans." She gave him a very sweet smile. "How about if we go together?"

"I don't dance very well."

"Nobody does."

So Randy warmed up to the idea and got his mom to do the driving. She liked Dina right away, especially since she's a straight-A student and babysits for three different families. Mrs. Mansfield said she had spirit and fortitude, and that it'd be great if some of that could rub off on Randy.

Lucy's mouth is slightly open, and she's making circles on her chin with a finger. The way Randy's just positioned his queen has left her with a difficult choice—retreat with her knight and surrender a bishop, or save the bishop and lose the knight. She reluctantly moves the bishop, which Randy was hoping she would do. He takes the knight. Within three moves, he has the bishop, too.

He takes another quick look at his brother's table and wonders if he's detecting some concern on Jenna McNulty's face. Zeke's expression is slightly smug, and Randy hopes he's smart enough not to get overconfident and blow it.

The way Randy sees it, Zeke is probably as smart as he is but manages to get blinded by ambition too often. And his arrogance never helps. When Randy takes a hard look at himself, he realizes that a certain degree of Zeke's conceit might not be a bad addition to his own repertoire. But the volume of ego that Zeke possesses—and their father, too—generally leads to a downfall.

Randy has figured out that he usually beats Zeke because Zeke is too stubborn to give each move the consideration it deserves. Zeke still tells himself—despite having beaten Randy only six times in their most recent one hundred matches (twenty-nine draws)—that defeating his brother simply shouldn't take a 100 percent effort. That Zeke is superior enough that his normal game will suffice.

Randy has his hands folded now and is looking kindly across the board at Lucy. She has two pawns and her king remaining, and Randy has her in check. She can get out of it this time, but on Randy's next move, one of his pawns will reach the end of the board and be promoted to queen. Lucy will be in checkmate.

She frowns, then looks up with a gracious smile. She tips her king onto its side in concession, lets out a sigh, and reaches her hand across the board.

Randy shakes her hand and they stand. He gives her a half hug with his arm around her shoulder and nods to the Regional Director.

Randy looks around and sees that neither of the other two games seems to be near completion. (Pramod has already won his.) He carefully turns the knob on the conference room door, and they step into the hallway.

"Great game," he says to Lucy.

"You throttled me."

The door reopens noisily, and Randy's father steps out. "You're on your way!" he says to Randy.

Randy shrugs. "Maybe."

"Listen to him," Mr. Mansfield says, turning to Lucy. "He's the man and he won't even admit it. The kid's going to win this thing."

Lucy gives him a tight smile. "He played very well."

"You said it." He points his thumb back toward the conference room. "Now we'll see how the other one measures up."

"He's playing Jenna?"

"Yep. I don't see why they don't have two different divisions. Men and ladies. Seems that'd be a lot fairer for you girls."

Lucy shifts her eyes just slightly and catches Randy's. "I think we're holding our own," she says.

"Sure. You gals are terrific. Best of luck to you." And he goes back into the room.

Randy puffs out his cheeks, and his eyes get wider. His dad always manages to stun him. "He's . . . excited," he says.

"He should be. You guys are doing great."

"Yeah. You gonna stick around?"

"Might as well. I'd love to see Pramod get his butt kicked in the semis."

"Wouldn't we all?"

The Malone match seems closest to a conclusion, so Randy keeps his eyes mostly on that one. Serena Leung has only her king and a rook, but Buddy is definitely in trouble. He still has a bishop and two pawns, but the bishop is in a useless position given how his king is trapped by Leung's pieces.

Leung puts Buddy in check with her rook, and Buddy makes the only move that he can, bringing his king to the first rank. Leung shifts her rook forward one space, resulting in check yet again. And Buddy responds with his only possible move, putting his king back where it was.

Leung lets out a sigh and says, "Perpetual check," which sounds like it might be a good thing, but all of the players know better. It means Malone has forced a draw. Leung can put him in check with every move, but Buddy can safely get out of it with the next one. And Buddy can't bring his bishop into play because he has to respond to every check.

With the right placement of material, such a frustrating scenario could go on forever.

So Malone has survived. They shake hands and agree to take the permissible five-minute break before starting over.

Randy notices that there are three and a half doughnuts still sitting on a tray near the windows. None of them look particularly appetizing—the ones with sprinkles or fillings are long gone—but he picks up an all-chocolate one with a gooey white glaze and takes a large bite while heading for the exit door.

It's fairly warm for a January day in Scranton, around thirty-six degrees and sunny. Pramod is standing on the walk in front of the hotel, talking on his cell phone. Serena Leung is sitting on a low cement wall about forty feet away, eyeing Pramod. Buddy is standing in the lobby, looking blankly out the window.

Randy nods to Buddy as he walks past, his mouth too full of doughnut to say anything.

"You win?" Malone asks.

Randy wipes his mouth with his sleeve and swallows. "Yeah. Barely."

"We gotta play all over again," he says, jutting his chin toward Serena.

"I saw."

"I never even heard of her."

"Me either."

"Your brother still in there?"

57

"Yeah."

They stand quietly for a minute, watching traffic on Jefferson veer off toward the Central Scranton Expressway. Pramod steps into the lobby and grins at Malone. He points to his watch and says, "What's the holdup?"

Buddy shakes his head. "She's good."

"The Shark Lady? You must be losing your touch. She's not even seeded."

"So what? She can play."

"Maybe I'll find out." Pramod smirks. "If you can't handle her, that is."

Randy steps toward the doors. "I'm gonna get some air."

"Can't believe that little kid's still in it," Pramod says, loud enough for Randy to hear.

Randy sits on the wall next to Serena, who's leaning forward with her elbows on her knees. She turns her head slightly toward him and squints.

"You seem to be surprising people," Randy says.

She gives him a defiant look. "How so?"

"Nobody expected any unseeded players to get this far."

She shrugs. "They were wrong."

"What grade are you in?"

"Eleven. What are you, like fifth?"

"Fifth seed?"

"Fifth *grade*."

"I'm in ninth," Randy says evenly. "And I *am* the fifth seed."

"Big deal."

"I didn't say it was."

She finally breaks into a reluctant smile. "That's right, you didn't. . . . Sorry. I can be a bitch."

"No problem."

"I mean, you *do* look very young."

"I know."

Malone taps on the window and gestures for Serena to come in.

"Back to the grind," she says.

"Do it up."

"I try."

Randy sits outside for another minute, until his ears get cold. Pramod is slumped on that leather couch in the lobby. "Sit down a second," he says.

Randy doesn't sit, but he stops next to the couch and looks at Pramod expectantly.

Pramod is staring at his fingernails again. "When you play Jenna, she'll definitely favor her queenside," he says.

"So?"

"So you need to know that. And you need to control the center."

"We *always* need to control the center. What do you care how I play her?"

"Because I want to win the tournament," Pramod says. "If you beat her in the semis, they might as well start putting my name on the trophy right then."

"I'll be sure to notify the engraver."

Serena catches Randy's eye as he tries to slip unnoticed into the conference room. Her rematch with Malone is several moves old, but neither player has taken any pieces.

Most eyes in the room are on Zeke's game against Jenna. Both players have the same material left: two pawns, a rook, and the king. It's Jenna's move, and she can take one of Zeke's pawns with a pawn of her own (hers are side by side near the center of the board) or capture his other pawn with her rook (which is just one space forward of its original position in the corner).

Capturing with the rook would be suicidal, because she would immediately lose it to Zeke's rook, which is shielded by the pawn but is in the same rank as Jenna's. But not taking that pawn would be equally fatal, because Zeke needs just one move to promote the pawn in question to a queen. And that would leave Jenna in checkmate. Either way, she's in deep trouble.

Randy quietly takes a seat next to his father. Jenna finds the best alternative and moves her rook to the opposite corner, putting Zeke in check. He can easily get out of it, but a cat-and-mouse game ensues, with Zeke moving his king up the board one space at a time and Jenna keeping him in check with her rook. This is not the perpetual check that Buddy Malone forced, since the position of the pieces changes with every move and he can eventually get out of check.

But the advantage clearly belongs to Zeke. He carefully circles the pawns with his king. If Jenna captures Zeke's lone pawn near the center, his next move would be to promote his remaining pawn to queen, assuring the victory.

Jenna is taking a long time to think, and Randy's already gone over every possible remaining move in his head. Unless Zeke makes a gigantic blunder, the game will be his within three or four moves.

Randy turns to his dad and mouths, "He's got it."

"How?" Mr. Mansfield mouths back.

"Just watch." Randy's whispering now. "She can't get out of it."

Jenna has a deep frown and seems to see the inevitable. Zeke captures both pawns with his king on consecutive moves. Jenna's last-ditch effort brings her rook all the way back, next to her king in the first rank. But two moves later she's in checkmate.

She looks bewildered, and so does Zeke, frankly. With the Malone-Leung match still progressing, there's no possibility of applause from the fifteen or so remaining spectators.

Mr. Mansfield points toward the door, and Randy and Zeke follow him out. No need to look at the brackets; it'll be Mansfield versus Mansfield in the semifinals.

"Yes!" Zeke says, pumping his fist when they're out of immediate earshot. "I took her down."

Mr. Mansfield holds out both palms and Zeke slaps them, then flips his palms over for his dad.

"She used that Sicilian Dragon bit, huh?" Randy says.

"Huh?" Zeke looks at him like he's crazy. "I don't know. Something like that. I'm starving."

"Yeah," Mr. Mansfield says. "You guys need to get refueled."

"I could see what she was doing after about three moves," Zeke says, ignoring Randy. "She thought she had this really elaborate opening, but it's the same game I play all the time. I saw it coming a mile away."

"See?" Mr. Mansfield says to Randy. "*Always* know your opponent."

"I figured it out in about two seconds," Zeke says. "As soon as she made her third move, I'm like, *That's the Sicilian thing.* She never had a chance after that."

"You got in her head," Mr. Mansfield says.

"I lived there."

■ SEVEN ■
Pushing Carts

The McDonald's on Washington Avenue is one of those urban storefront spots, not freestanding like most of its billion franchises, including the one back in Sturbridge. This one is long and narrow and wedged between a CVS drugstore and a jewelry shop across from the Lackawanna County Courthouse.

Mr. Mansfield gave Zeke a twenty to buy lunch and went over to the Steamtown Mall for something. So Randy and Zeke walked the four blocks to McDonald's, not saying anything till they got there.

Scranton is not a thriving city, and midday on a Saturday it seems particularly empty.

"I'm getting two fish sandwiches," Randy says as they wait

behind three college-age guys and a woman with no front teeth in a NASCAR jacket.

"Don't tell *me*," Zeke replies. "You think I'm ordering for you?"

"No. I'm just saying."

"Fish sucks."

"You don't have to eat it."

"I don't plan to."

Lunch was available at the hotel for all of the quarterfinalists, but few players took up the offer. Jenna McNulty seemed too stunned to eat, and Buddy Malone went straight to his room after losing his rematch. Serena Leung told Zeke she didn't want any possibility of having to eat with Pramod, who she'll meet in the semis. Silvio Vega was already on his way back to Wilkes-Barre.

When Zeke and Randy left, only Pramod and Lucy Ahada were dining at the hotel, sitting uncomfortably with the tournament officials as they munched on salads and turkey sandwiches.

Zeke orders a hamburger and Chicken McNuggets. The girl at the counter asks, "Will that be all?"

Zeke frowns and tilts his head toward Randy. "Whatever he wants, too."

They take a booth near the entrance, across the aisle from an apparently homeless guy who's staring blankly while nursing a cup of coffee. He has a scruffy white beard and black shoes with no laces in them.

Zeke watches as Randy unwraps one of his sandwiches and takes off the top of the bun. He grabs a couple of napkins and wipes a large glob of tartar sauce from it. "They always put way too much," Randy says.

"You could ask them to go light, you know."

"That never works. You ask for a special order and they mess it up some other way. Extra-cheeselate it or something."

Zeke pulls a limp pickle slice off his hamburger and sets it on the tray. "Like you could do better."

"Like I'd want to."

"You *do* have to get a job this summer, you know. Practice saying this: 'Hi, may I take your order?' Who else is gonna hire you?" Zeke has worked as a parking-lot shopping-cart collector the past three summers at Kmart. *Muscle work,* he thinks. *Great training.*

"I'll find a job," Randy says. "What do you care?"

"They made me work as soon as I turned fifteen," Zeke says. "No way you're sitting on your fat ass for another summer."

"I *said* I'd get a job."

"Men *work,*" Zeke says, imitating their father's stern, no-nonsense cadence.

Randy gives a snorty laugh. Then his face becomes expressionless and he squints, slowly raising his hand and pointing toward his eye. "Game face," he says.

Zeke laughs. "He gave you that shit, too?"

"It's our best weapon."

Zeke looks down and shakes his head slowly. "There's something to all that, you know."

"Yeah. Something. But you can't just will yourself to overpower somebody who's smarter than you are."

"You can cut down the odds a little," Zeke says. "I just beat the hell out of the top seed. Part of that was because I intimidated her."

"Maybe you outsmarted her."

Zeke blows some air out the side of his mouth in a puffy sound. "I think she choked."

"It happens."

"She's probably crying her eyes out. Can't believe she lost to some peasant from Sturbridge."

"Bet Malone isn't feeling too good either."

"Anyway," Zeke says, "you can't overpower everybody. Dad thinks you have to be ruthless about *everything*. He doesn't even see what it costs him."

"Like what?"

Zeke's eyes get wider. "Respect. I mean, nobody really says anything, but you can tell people think he's an asshole. Like back when he was coaching us when we were little? He'd always rather win than have fun. The other parents saw right through that. Except the few who were even bigger jerks than he is."

Zeke picks up a McNugget and turns it around, frowning at it. "Nobody cares if a six-year-old wins a T-ball game."

Randy just nods.

"Then when it matters—like in high school sports or this tournament—it's the same thing as far as he's concerned. Always about adding some notch in the belt."

Randy looks stunned. "You're actually admitting that?"

Zeke thinks for a second. He's never been open with Randy about their father. He's figured that since he's been the beneficiary of the man's lack of objectivity, why worry about how he treats Randy?

"So what else does it cost him?" Randy asks.

Zeke turns away. The homeless guy is looking at them. "You want these?" Zeke asks him, pointing to the three Mc-Nuggets he hasn't eaten.

"All right," the guy says.

Zeke wraps them in a napkin and walks over.

"Thank you," the man says.

"No problem."

Zeke sits back down and lets out his breath. "Mom's pretty much had it with him," he says.

"Yeah?"

"You think he drives *us* crazy? You listen to him lately? He says she's wearing out the tires because she brakes too much going down hills. And he got diarrhea last week because she didn't wash the lettuce good enough. And *you* only got a B plus in Spanish last semester because she lets you watch too much TV."

"He blamed that on her?"

"It's such bullshit," Zeke says. "He constantly tells us we have to take total responsibility for our actions, but he never does. It's always somebody else's fault."

"You do that, too, you know."

"Like when?"

"All the time."

"Everybody does." Zeke tries not to smile but doesn't completely succeed. "Dad thinks he never gets to be vice president because his boss is a dick. So he keeps whining in the same shit job instead of working at some other bank."

"When does he tell you these things?"

"He doesn't. But I hear him bitching to Mom all the time."

67

"I guess I need to pay more attention."

"Yeah," Zeke says. "Start acting like a *man*."

"Yes, Daddy."

"He's right about that one."

"Shut up."

"Make me."

The door opens and Jenna walks in, carrying her briefcase.

"Well, well," she says, smiling broadly and stopping next to the booth. "Didn't think I'd find you two together."

"Why not?" Zeke says.

"Big showdown this afternoon."

"We gotta eat," Randy says. "No way we were eating with Pramod."

"Right. Shove over."

Randy slides toward the wall, and Jenna sits across from Zeke. "Pramod will have his hands full with Serena," she says. "She's the real thing."

"You've played her?" Zeke asks.

"I *taught* her. They had this clinic at the library last summer. Three afternoons. Serena comes in dressed like a"—Jenna turns her head and looks across the aisle, where the homeless guy has finished the McNuggets and has returned his blank stare to the window; she lowers her voice—"like a street person. But she turns out to be brilliant. And her family's regular; she just has this freakish attitude. Anyway, she's a prodigy. She just has no idea that she is. This is her first tournament ever, and she might just win it."

Zeke is staring openmouthed at Jenna. Randy lifts his foot and nudges Zeke's shin. Zeke sits up a bit straighter and closes his mouth.

"You think she'll beat Pramod?" Randy asks.

"She might." Jenna steps out of the booth and raps her fingers on the table. "Then one of you would have to take her on."

"Either way," Zeke says. "It doesn't matter who we play."

"Yeah," she says, "but which one of you will it be?"

Randy and Zeke stare at each other for a second. Randy points to his eye again. "Whichever one is tougher, I guess."

Jenna nods toward the counter. "Time to indulge," she says. "I only eat french fries after I lose."

"Been a while, huh?" Randy asks.

"Yeah," she says, "but a couple of times a year won't kill me."

Zeke turns and watches her go. When he turns back, Randy says, "Nice, huh?"

Zeke blushes a bit. "She's okay." He balls up his hamburger wrapper and sets it down on the tray. "You want anything else?"

"I'd drink a milk shake."

"Vanilla?"

"Yeah. Why? You getting it?"

"Sure," Zeke says, staring at Jenna. He gets up and stands next to her on line.

That's the only reason Randy can figure why Zeke would offer to get him anything.

It occurs to Randy for the first time that he might actually win this tournament. The odds are strong that he'll beat Zeke as usual, and who knows what would happen in the final? He'd like nothing more than to silence Pramod. And if Serena knocks Pramod out first, then Randy would have to be considered the favorite. Even against a prodigy.

But Zeke won't be beaten easily. There's too much at stake for him not to play his best game. He'll be focused and intense, and he'll do his best to intimidate Randy. And Zeke is one of the few people who can actually pull it off. He gets that from all those sports that he plays. Randy envies that a little. He dropped out of sports early.

There *was* that last season of organized basketball back in sixth grade. It wasn't the school team but another recreational program at the Y. Still, the competition was intense, and most of the better players who *were* on the school team played in this league, too.

So when Randy's dad assigned him to cover Peter Adams in the fourth game—five-ten, 168-pound Peter Adams— Randy could see the beginning of the end. By the first time-out, Peter had six points and three rebounds, and Mr. Mansfield clapped his fists over Randy's ears and said, "Box him *out!* Be a man and get in his face!"

The opposing coach had the decency to switch to a zone and played Peter for only half the game, but his team still won by twenty points.

Fortunately for Randy, there were only four games left. He low-keyed it in the two games he played and was too "sick" with a cold to participate in the other two. His father was totally disgusted with him about it.

Zeke and Jenna come back with supersize containers of fries and set them on the tray. "Have some," Jenna says, sitting next to Randy again.

"Brain food?"

"Solace," she says. "Some comfort after that butt kicking your brother gave me."

Randy takes two fries and asks, "Where's my shake?"

Zeke looks at Jenna. "Damn."

"I'll go," Randy says. "Gimme some money."

Zeke hands him a five, and Jenna slides out of the booth to let Randy by.

The counter is busy, and only one register is open. The girl is frantically bagging orders. "We need fries!" she yells to someone in the back.

When Randy orders, she says, "The shake machine isn't working too well. The chocolate's okay, but the vanilla is kind of syrupy . . . and gray."

"Chocolate will be fine."

Jenna is laughing when Randy returns. Could Zeke have actually said something witty? Most of the fries are gone, too.

"Maybe I'll Kmartulate this summer after all," Randy says.

"It's hard as hell pushing those carts around," Zeke says. "Especially in July when it's ninety."

"Yeah, well, I figure maybe it'd be good for me."

Zeke turns to Jenna. "Suddenly he's got ambition."

"No," Randy says. "Suddenly I'd rather do anything than work at a McDonald's."

"Where do *you* work?" Zeke asks Jenna.

"I tutor. Last summer I waitressed, but this year we're going to Spain."

"We?"

"My parents. It's a graduation present."

"Oh," Zeke says. "I'll be lucky if I get a card."

71

Jenna takes a Wet-Nap from her pocket and wipes the grease and salt off her fingers. "You guys must play each other every day, huh?"

Randy wipes his fingers on his pants. "No. Just once in a while."

"So who's gonna win today?"

"How would we know?" Randy says.

"That's why they play the games," Zeke says. "To find out."

"Who *usually* wins?"

Zeke shoots a cold look at his brother. "Depends," he says. "If I give a shit and pay attention, I win."

Randy rolls his eyes slightly but says nothing. There's some truth in that, and he knows it. Zeke probably cares enough only about 5 percent of the time, but this afternoon will certainly be one of those games.

■ EIGHT ■
Two Nights' Sleep

With another half hour to kill before the semifinals, Randy starts toward the hotel elevator. Zeke is actually carrying on a conversation with Jenna in the lobby, and the boys' father has not reappeared.

Randy sees his mother—a heavyset woman with striking eyebrows and bronze-tinted hair—rapidly approaching the hotel's main entrance. Trailing behind her is Randy's girlfriend, Dina, walking somewhat awkwardly due to her platform heels. He feels a bit of warmth spreading across his cheeks—these two people actually get his sense of humor; they actually *have* senses of humor. And they're kind to him, in direct contrast to the men in his life.

He gives a wave, slicing the air sideways with his hand. "Hey, Mom."

"Are you still playing?" she asks, somewhat teasingly. "Or did we drive over here for nothing?"

"Not nothing. We're both still in it." He steps over to Dina and kisses her. "How you doing?" he asks her.

"My mom . . . didn't really know why I was coming over here," she says somewhat slowly. "She's like, 'How do you watch chess?' And I'm trying to explain to her that I'm not really watching *chess* so much as watching how you're *doing* at chess?"

Randy pats her head and she giggles. "Well put," he says.

Dina's mother was born in the Dominican Republic and grew up in New York City. Her father is an auto mechanic, and he's lived his entire life in Sturbridge. They met in Shorty's Bar on Main Street and never married, but they've lived together for fifteen years.

"I said it's so very much more interesting when your boyfriend is playing than when *other* people play," Dina says.

"So very much more interesting," Randy repeats. "That's like two adverbs and three adjectives."

"So?" She blushes with a shy smile. "I'm very descriptive. I brought my camera."

"To record this for posterity?"

"And for the school paper. My English teacher wants me to write for it."

"About this tournament?"

"Mostly about the new computers in the library."

"I guess that would be so very much more interesting than chess."

"But a picture of you playing *would* be interesting."

"Especially since I'm playing against Zeke."

"Against Zeke?" Mrs. Mansfield says. "They're making you play against each *other*?"

"There's only four of us left. Sooner or later we had to face each other if we kept winning."

"That'll go over big with your father," Mrs. Mansfield says with a dose of sarcasm. "He won't have an opponent to hate."

"You never know," Randy says. "He might end up despising both of us."

"How does Zeke feel about this?"

"Same as he feels about everything."

"What do you mean?"

"That his great superiority will shine through and he'll clobber me."

Dina grabs Randy's arm lightly. "He says I have good ideas but I don't present them coherently."

"Zeke does?"

"No! Mr. Chandless." Her English teacher. "He says writing for the newspaper will help me to straighten out my thoughts."

"That could be dangerous."

"You think?"

"Who is Zeke talking to?" Mrs. Mansfield asks, looking across the lobby.

"She was supposed to win the tournament."

"She's very pretty."

"He beat her this morning."

Mrs. Mansfield lifts her painted eyebrows. "I should go over and say hello."

Randy considers this, then says, "How about seeing my room first?" He knows that Zeke is possibly on the verge of his second breakthrough of the day, and something within Randy wants to cut his brother a break and steer his mother away. "It'll just take a minute."

"All right," she says, and she follows Randy toward the elevator. Dina follows Mrs. Mansfield.

"It's on the third floor," Randy says.

"This place is *nice*," Dina says, running her hand along the bright steel wall of the elevator.

"Never been in an elevator before?" Randy asks with a grin.

"I mean the *hotel*. It's a lot nicer than the rest of the neighborhood."

"They've entirely de-Scrantonized it."

"Is that good?"

"I don't know. We passed a bunch of beautiful old buildings when we walked to McDonald's. A lot of the storefronts are empty, though."

"They're supposedly very high-tech," Dina says as the elevator stops at the third floor.

"The storefronts?"

"The computers."

"What computers?"

"At *school*. The ones I'm writing about for the paper."

"Oh yeah." Randy laughs. "Those."

"I already took a picture of one of them. Except Bobby Colaneri was sitting at it, and I think he was giving the finger."

"You *think*?"

76

"His hand was on the mouse, and I'm thinking that I'm pretty sure he had his middle finger sticking up. But I haven't looked real closely at it yet, so I don't know for sure."

"That'd be great."

"Not for me it wouldn't. My first published photograph?"

"It'd be a classic."

Randy opens the hotel room door and says, "This is it."

"Were you . . . able to sleep all right?" Mrs. Mansfield asks.

"Yeah, I wasn't scared." He says it with a "Don't baby me, Mom" tone.

"Did you sleep in both beds?" she asks, noticing that both sets of blankets and sheets are mussed.

"At the same time. Actually, I went back and forth, five minutes in one bed, five minutes in the other. It was like getting two nights' sleep at once."

Dina sits on the bed closer to the door and bounces a bit.

Mrs. Mansfield goes into the bathroom and closes the door. Randy sits next to Dina and starts bouncing, too.

"So, how was it last night?" Dina asks.

"Lonely," Randy says, but his tone is teasing. He puts his arms around Dina, and they fall back, kissing. "Would have been great if you'd been along," he whispers.

"Like we could have pulled *that* off," Dina says with a smile.

The bathroom door opens, and they sit up with a start. Mrs. Mansfield raises her eyebrows but doesn't say anything.

"Zeke—" Randy catches himself starting to explain why the second bed was used and decides to cut his brother yet another break. "Zeke played really well this morning."

"I'm not surprised," Mrs. Mansfield says. "Your father made such a big deal about it all week that Zeke was probably petrified of losing."

"That wouldn't have helped."

"No, but it's your father's way. Make everybody so tense that they either overachieve or crack."

"That's me," Randy says. "Overachieving in everything."

Mrs. Mansfield smiles. "Name one thing."

Dina laughs. "Ever achieving in overything."

"*Never* achieving in anerything," Randy says. "Until today, that is." He flexes his bicep. "Mr. Chess, they'll call me. King of the Scranton frontier."

Zeke is astonishing himself today, not because he's advanced so far in the tournament but because he's managed to hold a conversation with Jenna McNulty for nearly half an hour.

She's done most of the talking—about politics and women's professional tennis and her rigid educator parents (he's the principal of a junior high school, and she teaches American literature at Wilkes)—but he's thrown in a few self-deprecating lines about himself and a couple of jabs at Pramod.

"I can't wait to see him go down in the final," Zeke says. "He's such an egotist."

"So you expect to be watching?" Jenna asks.

"I didn't mean *that*."

"He's good, huh?"

"Pramod?"

"Randy."

Zeke gives a slight scowl, but then he adds a half nod. "I can beat him."

"You beat me."

"Your game is sort of similar to his, so . . ." Zeke shrugs. "That helped, I guess."

"Well, believe me, everybody in the tournament is hoping one of you will kick Pramod's ass."

Zeke discovers that he and Jenna do have a few things in common. She says she sometimes wonders if her drive to excel in school and chess and other pursuits is more her parents' need than her own.

So Zeke's feeling more confident than ever when his mother and brother and Dina walk over. "This is my mom," he says, pointing to her, even though she's inches away.

Jenna sticks out her hand and gives her name. She smiles at Dina.

"And this is my brother's girlfriend, Dina," Zeke says, putting his hand up and almost touching Dina's shoulder. It's the first time he's ever said her name aloud; first time he's ever smiled at her.

"I heard you're a very good chess player," Dina says to Jenna.

"Not as good as Zeke was this morning."

"They're both amazing at it," Dina says. She giggles. "I watch them play against each other sometimes, and it's *so* intense. Like all of their *man*hood is on the line."

"Do you play?"

"I know *how* to play, but Randy gets frustrated at me

79

because he knows it so well that he doesn't want to wait for me to figure things out for myself."

"I'll help you," Zeke says, making a supreme effort to be charming while Jenna's standing there. "Randy's not detached enough to be objective."

"Oh, I'm detached," Randy says with mock huffiness. "She just needs gumption and intimidation. That's what it's all about, right?"

As if on cue, Mr. Mansfield enters the lobby. "What are you two doing?" he asks, shifting his eyes from Randy to Zeke and ignoring everyone else.

"Hanging out," Randy says.

"Socializing," says Zeke.

Mr. Mansfield checks his watch. "Don't you think you're being a bit too nonchalant here?"

"We're *very* chalant, Dad," Randy says.

"Ought to be getting ready, don't you think?"

"We *are* ready," Zeke says.

"Come over here, you two." He gestures toward the conference room, then turns to his wife. "Where did you park?"

"In the *parking lot*, Ernie."

"Did you lock the doors?"

"Yes," she says coldly.

"Might want to go out and double-check." He walks away, and the boys follow him past the conference room, into a narrow hallway.

"Do you think the Knicks stand around with a bunch of girls a few minutes before a play-off game?" he asks. "You think the Giants hang out with the cheerleaders at halftime?"

Zeke leans against the wall and scowls. Randy looks down at his shoes.

"It's ten minutes to one," Mr. Mansfield says. "The party's over. I suggest you get in there and prepare yourselves for battle."

■ NINE ■
Pinned to the Bishop

Randy swallows hard as he enters the conference room. The folding chairs for spectators have been rearranged in a semi-circle facing the two tables, so he'll definitely be in the spot-light now.

The Regional Director is in the seat farthest from the en-trance, shuffling through some papers. He nods to the boys as they enter the room. "Did you get some lunch?" he asks. "Why don't you two take this table"—the one on the left—"and we'll get started in a few minutes."

Randy sits. He feels small and young suddenly, about to be a victim of the intimidation factor he's been joking about all morning. He looks at his brother, who's staring out the window. Zeke's been decent to him over the past hour or so, but that can't last, and Randy knows it.

There's too much on the line for that.

Serena is the next one to enter the room. She takes the seat on the same side of her board as Randy is on his. "Nervous?" she asks.

"Some."

"You look it."

"How so?"

"I don't know," Serena says. "Pale. How do you describe when a person looks scared? Maybe you just feel it."

"You don't look scared."

She shrugs. "Maybe I learned how to hide it."

Randy takes off his corduroy shirt and hangs it over the back of his chair. He notices that a bruise is starting to develop on his bicep, where his father jabbed him with his thumb earlier.

"This guy I'm playing against is a prick," Serena says.

Randy would usually say the same thing about his brother. Something between them seems to have shifted since yesterday, though. Not much, but a little. "One of us is going to knock him out," Randy says.

"*Literally*, if I had the chance," Serena says, smiling wickedly. "But if I can just bump his sorry ass out of the tournament, I'll be happy."

The audience now consists of the Mansfield parents, Dina, the Regional Director and his assistant, Lucy Ahada, Jenna McNulty, and Jenna's parents, who arrived minutes before, expecting to watch their daughter in the semifinals and the final.

Randy, playing white, opens by moving the pawn in front of his king two spaces forward to e4. Zeke brings the pawn in front of his queenside bishop forward just one space and stares across the board until Randy finally meets his eyes.

Randy knows that Zeke will often make a seemingly careless move early in the game. The strategy is to leave the opponent with a *He must know something I don't know* bewilderment.

Randy continues on a traditional course and moves a second pawn to the center, one space to the left of his first. Zeke then moves a pawn two spaces forward, setting up a situation where Randy can take that pawn and Zeke would follow by taking Randy's.

Randy decides that the exchange of pawns won't hurt him, so he takes the bait.

The brothers move quickly, exchanging a fair amount of material and working the edges of the board more than most experts would recommend. Ten minutes into the game, Randy snares a pawn with one of his knights, then grimaces and fights back a feeling of dread when he realizes that he's about to lose his queen.

As a defensive ploy, Randy looks casually at another of his pawns, which has been left under attack by the shifting of the knight. Zeke can safely take the pawn with a rook. Randy winces slightly, hoping Zeke will follow his gaze and fail to notice that the bishop can take the white queen.

But Zeke puts a finger atop the bishop. A familiar, distinct whisper breaks the silence. "That's the one."

All eyes turn to Mr. Mansfield, who keeps his gaze firmly focused on the board. Pramod smiles and shakes his head slowly while Serena glares over.

Zeke frowns as he moves the bishop and takes Randy's queen. The Regional Director tips his head toward his assistant, and they exchange a few barely audible words. Zeke smacks the button on the clock and faces Randy with a sour look.

Mr. Mansfield's coaching would have had no effect. Zeke had already touched the bishop, so he had to move it anyway. And both boys are far better players than their father, so neither would pay him any attention.

Randy spends longer than usual pondering his move, since Zeke now has a clear advantage. Randy's been in stickier situations against Zeke and worked his way out, but never with so much on the line.

Zeke slows the pace as well, but his next several moves are steady and tactical, increasing the likelihood that he'll win.

Randy's remaining rook is being attacked and is pinned to his bishop, so he knows that he'll be losing another piece. He considers his options for the coming moves, then reaches for the rook.

"No."

Randy lets out his breath in a huff and looks straight up at the ceiling. This time Pramod laughs loud enough for everyone to hear. The Regional Director and his assistant rise from their chairs and walk over to the Mansfield boys.

Dr. Kerrigan reaches for the clock and stops it.

Mr. Mansfield has also stood up and has his arms folded tightly. "What's the problem?" he barks.

The Director turns to Pramod and Serena and says, "Please continue your game." He motions with his fingers for the three Mansfields to follow him into the hallway.

"Normally, this would be clear grounds for disqualification," he says.

"What would be?" Mr. Mansfield says. "They're *both* my sons."

"Yes, I know that. And you appeared to be trying to coach them both."

"I wasn't coaching anybody."

"You gave direction to both players. Rather fervently the second time."

"Like hell I did," Mr. Mansfield says. "Besides, they're my *kids*."

"Dad," Randy says, "can you tone it down?"

"Shut *up*, Randy!" he shouts. "I'll handle this."

"Leave him alone, Dad," Zeke says. "It's our game, let *us* handle it."

"You wanna handle it? Fine. Let's see you handle it."

"I was winning the frickin' match, Dad."

"You better have."

The Regional Director turns in such a way that he and his assistant and Randy and Zeke form a sort of circle, with Mr. Mansfield on the outside. "What do you boys think about this?" he asks.

"I think we should just finish the game," Zeke says.

Randy nods in agreement. "So do I."

The assistant sticks his thumbnail between his top front teeth and makes a clicking sound with his tongue. "Normally, there would be a disqualification."

86

"You guys already said that," Zeke says.

"You can't disqualify them both!" Mr. Mansfield says.

"Yes, we can. The question is, should we?"

"This is bullshit."

"The rules are very clear."

"Rules, my ass."

Zeke puts his hand firmly on his father's chest. "You're not helping," he says.

"Fine." Mr. Mansfield throws his hands into the air and walks away. "You geniuses figure it out." They all watch as he walks toward the entrance, lighting a cigarette before he goes out.

The Director shakes his head and forces a smile. "I'd be willing to abort that game and have you boys start over. But if there's another incident, we'll have to disqualify you both."

"We didn't do anything!" Zeke says, his voice rising.

"That's true," says the Director. "But the integrity of the tournament demands that we follow the protocol. And we're definitely bending it if we continue."

Zeke lets out a sigh and directs his next comment to Randy. "I was winning."

Randy knows that it's true. But it isn't his fault that their father is out of control.

Zeke shrugs and actually starts to laugh. "Let's start over then."

"It's the best decision under the circumstances," the Director says.

"The only fair way," says his assistant.

Mrs. Mansfield comes quietly out of the conference room. "Is everything all right?" she asks.

"Fine," Zeke says. "Dad just cost me the tournament, that's all."

"Where is he?" Her tone suggests that she's ready to rip him to shreds.

"He went outside. Do us all a favor and make sure he doesn't come back, please."

"You can count on it."

Dina has come out to the lobby, too. She follows Randy and Zeke. "Did you really go back and forth to two different beds last night?" she asks.

"Just one," Randy says. "I let a homeless guy use the other."

"That's nice." Dina giggles again.

Zeke stops at the conference room door. "Can we get ten minutes?" he asks the Regional Director.

"Considering the circumstances, why don't you take fifteen?"

"I'm going to my room," Zeke says, heading for the elevator.

"Me too," says Randy.

Dina starts to follow, then flops down on the leather couch.

"Can you believe this shit?" Zeke says after pushing the 3 on the elevator panel.

Randy thinks it over, scrunches up his face, and says, "Yes."

They hustle down the hallway. Randy turns on the TV and sits on the edge of his bed, watching a Syracuse-Providence college basketball game. Within seconds, there's a knock on the door.

It's Zeke. "Forgot my key again," he says. "Can I use your bathroom?"

"Considering the circumstances, come on in."

"I was this close to punching that bastard."

"The Director?"

"*Dad*," Zeke says sharply. "What an idiot."

"He'd deck you right there."

"He could *try*." Zeke's face is red, and he wipes at his eye with his thumb.

"Come on," Randy says. The idea of his father and Zeke in a fistfight turns Randy's stomach. There's always been tension—a growing tension in every relationship in the house—but this is the first real threat that one of those relationships would burst like a pimple full of pus. And the domino effect would be immediate—Mom would get Dad kicked out of the house. The resentment on all sides would explode.

"Calm down," Randy says. "You just have to put up with the guy for a few more months."

"As soon as I graduate, I'm out of there."

"Yeah, but think about *me* for once. I've got three and a half years of high school left."

"And you want him around the whole time?" Zeke asks. "He's a dick."

"Not completely."

"Pretty close. . . . Do you actually think it would be better to keep things the way they are? Total denial?"

"Not denial," Randy says. "Just a balance."

"That's like perpetual check."

"Isn't that better than losing?"

"Not the way I play."

Randy thinks this over for a second. Zeke takes risks and they rarely pay off. But maybe when one does, it makes the bigger payoff worth it. Randy doesn't have enough confidence to test that theory himself. "Life's not a game," he says.

"Bull*shit* it isn't. And take a look around, brother. Every person you know is playing by different rules."

Zeke goes into the bathroom. Randy can hear him blowing his nose. He steps over to the window and looks out at Scranton, the blond-brick university buildings to the right, some seedy bars and deteriorating storefronts to the left. Just below, in the hotel parking lot, he can see his parents standing next to his father's car. Actually, his dad is leaning against the car, his arms folded and his expression dark as Mrs. Mansfield gives him hell. She's got a finger in his face, and her own face looks puffy and mean.

Mr. Mansfield swats the finger away from his chin and stands up straighter, arguing back.

Randy feels his shoulders sag and he shudders, sniffing hard as his eyes start to water.

"What are you looking at?" Zeke asks.

Randy just shakes his head. Zeke joins him at the window and sighs.

"We're in the middle of a tournament," Zeke says. "In the middle of the most important match of our lives, and we have to put up with this again? Like we're supposed to concentrate on *chess*?"

Randy lets out his breath and sits on the bed again.

"This is ridiculous," Zeke says, sitting next to Randy.

They watch the basketball game for several minutes,

not paying attention at all. Zeke mentions a couple of ways he might have told his father off. "Go give yourself a pep talk" or "Find a mirror and stare yourself down." He laughs bitterly the first time, but with some actual humor the second.

Randy can feel Zeke's anger subsiding, and he starts to feel slightly more at ease. He clears his throat. "I suppose if one of us wins the tournament, there'll be a huge parade back in Sturbridge."

"Absolutely," Zeke says, cracking a smile. "In Dad's honor, mostly."

"Of course. He's the whole reason for our success."

"I'd like to ride on a huge float and toss candy to all the children lining Main Street. And have the entire cheer-leading squad on the float with me and the marching band behind us."

"Well," Randy says, "if I win, I want to be in one of those old-time fire engines pulled by six horses. With fireworks going off in the sky and some really huge rock band coming in for the occasion."

"It'll be the biggest event in Sturbridge history. Because chess is *huge*, as you know."

"Everybody's into it."

"I can't think of anything bigger," Zeke says.

"Which is what makes us so special."

Zeke points at the television, where a Syracuse player has just dunked the ball and is running up the court. "You and Dina want to go to a game on Tuesday?"

"What game? With *you*?"

"Sturbridge at Scranton Prep."

"Wait a minute. You want me and Dina to come all the way back over here, with *you*, for a basketball game?"

"Why not?"

"Because you can't stand either one of us."

"Yes I can."

Randy thinks this over. Obviously, Jenna must have said something about being at the game. Obviously, Jenna feels comfortable around Randy, so obviously, he could help smooth the way for Zeke. "Just brotherly love, huh?"

Zeke frowns, but his face is brighter. "You're not so bad. And, yeah, it would make a better impression. She's kind of . . ."

Randy flicks up his eyebrows. "Above us?"

"No. Just mature. More like an adult."

"Well, maybe she has role models."

"Unlike us."

"Exactly."

When they get back to the lobby, Pramod is standing by the elevator. "Make it quick, boys," he says. "I'll be waiting in my room to be summoned."

"Don't hold your breath," Zeke says. "This may take a while."

"Tell you what," Pramod says. "Skip the semifinal. Set up two tables and I'll beat you both at the same time."

"Sure you will," Randy says. "Get over yourself, Pramod."

"Up yours," Pramod says. "I'll be taking a nap."

They start walking toward the conference room, but Zeke grabs Randy's arm and they stop. "You think maybe you could help me with something this winter?"

"Like what?" Randy asks.

"I was lifting weights the other day at the Y. Julie asked me if I'd coach in the indoor soccer league and I said I didn't think so, but now I'm thinking it might not be a bad idea."

"What age?"

"Kindergarten and first graders. Two afternoons a week."

Randy looks questioningly at Zeke, but he doesn't see any of the usual guile or derisiveness. "I think I could do that," he says. "I think that might be fun."

"I'll call her Monday. We'll make *sure* it's fun, believe me."

Mrs. Mansfield is sitting with Dina on the sofa, managing to look both annoyed and embarrassed. The boys' dad is not around. The four of them walk single file into the conference room with Zeke leading the way.

"Maybe Dad should adopt Pramod," Randy says as they take their seats.

"That would make him very happy," Zeke says. "He'd have a son to be proud of."

Serena Leung, who'd been sitting by the window with a scowl, steps over to the table.

"He cut you down, huh?" Randy asks.

"Yeah, well, I got *distracted*."

"Sorry about that."

Serena shakes her head slowly with a smile of resignation. "These children who can't control their parents."

"We suck."

"Well," Serena says, "kick his ass, whichever one of you gets the chance. I'm leaving."

"I will," Zeke says.

"No," Randy says, "I will." But he does feel genuinely bad

for Zeke, who was outplaying him in the first game and probably deserved to win. Randy would never throw a game, and he
knows that disruptions are a part of any competition. But he
keeps glancing at the door and hoping that his father won't
open it and come in.

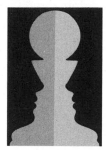

■ TEN ■
Small Disadvantages

Neither brother decides on a particularly aggressive opening. Zeke has the same empty, doomsday feeling in his gut as he did when Abington scored on that penalty kick last fall. As if his one real chance has slipped away again. He knows that the odds of beating Randy twice in a row (he's counting that first game as a victory) aren't good.

That feeling begins to dissipate as the game unfolds and neither player takes control. If Randy was going to trample him, it would have been evident right away.

Of all the people Zeke's tried to unnerve over the years, Randy's always been the most frustrating. Zeke *is* a good athlete, way better than average, the type who was always a leader on the youth soccer teams that transcended the local recreation programs, playing in weekend leagues against other select teams, participating in tournaments up in Binghamton and as far south as Philadelphia and Harrisburg. He saw significant playing time on the high school varsity as a freshman and was a starter at forward for three straight seasons. He also made first-team all-league in tennis last spring and is always an early selection for pickup basketball games and softball.

But there were better soccer players in those leagues, guys who could make him look slow and awkward as they slipped by with dazzling footwork and moves. And even if Zeke was probably in the top 10 percent of all high school tennis players in the state, there were dozens of guys who could beat him in straight sets at love without even breaking a sweat.

So Zeke knew very well what his father and his coaches were all too willing to ignore. Being very good is one thing; pretending to yourself that you have elite status just diminishes your actual worth.

Zeke is too good at pretending. But he's finally beginning to recognize that.

He studies the board. He knows that Randy's most recent move was meant to lure him into a rapid-fire exchange of pieces. He quickly envisions what the board would look like after each move, and how each player would almost surely have to react. He shifts a pawn one space forward.

Randy presses two fingers to his lower lip, glances up at his brother, and takes one of Zeke's rooks with one of his own.

Zeke captures that rook with a knight, Randy takes the knight with a pawn, and the next several moves go just as he expected. The exchanges continue until both players have lost a rook, a knight, and two pawns on consecutive moves. But Randy captures a third pawn on the final move of the series, coming away from the carnage with that slight advantage in material.

The once-sedate game is suddenly wide open. Dina sneezes. Zeke looks up at her quickly and returns his gaze to the board.

Zeke was at that dance in October, leaning back on the lowest row of the bleachers with his arms crossed. A few of his soccer teammates were there, but Zeke wasn't paying much attention to them. He was watching a group of girls dancing together near the deejay. He was trying not to look like he was watching, but he was.

In walks Randy, of all people, holding hands with a girl that Zeke couldn't quite bring himself to admit was rather cute.

People were going over to Randy and his date, joking around, laughing. After a few minutes, Randy and the girl started dancing. They kept at it for quite some time, mostly dancing fast but then doing a couple of slow ones.

"This is the lamest thing I've ever been to in my life," Zeke finally said to Donny Curtis, the goalie. "I'm out of here."

He drove down to the Turkey Hill convenience store and bought a pack of Yodels, then went home and watched three episodes of *The Simpsons* on DVD. *Anybody could get a girlfriend like that one*, he told himself, even though he'd never had one of his own.

Randy takes Zeke's remaining bishop with a knight, leaving the knight under attack by a pawn. Zeke winces slightly and takes the knight, but it wasn't quite an even exchange of pieces. There's the age-old argument of whether a bishop outranks a knight. But Zeke knows that—in Randy's hands at least—it does.

It's another of those small disadvantages that Zeke knows he can't afford. He'd been winning that first game because of a couple of big hits, most notably knocking out Randy's queen in the early going. But this one is turning into a slow battle of attrition, and that always falls to Randy's favor. Those small cuts eventually bleed you dry. And Zeke's got more cuts than Randy does.

The coaches at both Bloomsburg and Kutztown have said he can try out if he gets admitted, but there wouldn't be more than two or three roster spots for walk-ons at either school. Zeke desperately wants to continue playing soccer in college, so a season at a local two-year school like Lackawanna might be a better bet. But then what would he do about housing? Commute to Scranton? Keep living with his parents? There has to be a better alternative.

Having his father telling him what a star he is for all those years hasn't been a plus after all. Somehow it made him decide that an extra hour of working on his ball control was plenty, no need to make it two; that fifty sit-ups after practice were just as good as a hundred; that sometimes it wasn't worth running hills in the pouring rain. He was great; he was unbelievable. His natural talent would carry him as far as he wanted to go. It was heady stuff at twelve or thirteen or fifteen.

Randy never got caught up in all that, despite how outstanding he'd been when he was little. He never wanted to do that hard work, so he had no reason to pretend that he was anything other than what he was. He had no reason to try to fulfill some image his father had of him. No reason to be anybody but himself.

The game has been brutal, but Zeke has virtually no way to win it. His only real hope is a draw, to lure Randy into a stalemate.

Randy has been moving his last remaining pawn up the board toward promotion. Zeke's king and his lone pawn are stacked on the edge of the board, with the king in the seventh rank and the pawn one spot in front of it. Randy's king is in the next spot in that file, blocking Zeke's pawn from moving.

Randy advances his pawn. It's three spaces to the side of Zeke's king and one move away from promotion.

Zeke shifts the king one space to the side, still protecting his pawn. Randy promotes his pawn, then leans back to make a decision.

Zeke quickly reviews all of Randy's possible exchanges. The queen is nearly always the right choice for promotion, but is it in this case? A knight would put Zeke in immediate check, but he'd have five different moves to get out of it. Only one of those moves would really make sense, because he still needs to protect his pawn from Randy's king. And then Randy's advantage would be slimmer, because checkmating with just a knight and a king is difficult.

But the queen's dexterity can backfire in a case like this, too easily putting the king in a spot where it is not in checkmate but has no legal moves. Stalemate means starting over. Again.

It'd serve Pramod right to have to wait another hour, Zeke thinks. But Randy does the logical thing and promotes to a queen.

Zeke has just one legal move, and he shifts the king to his right. Randy brings the queen into the same rank.

Zeke moves his king to the corner of the board, three spaces down from Randy's king. That exposes his pawn, of course, and Randy takes it with his king.

There is only one move Zeke can make. He shifts his king to the left.

Randy gives a tight smile, nods to his brother, and moves his queen directly in front of Zeke's king, protected by his own.

Checkmate.

Zeke lets out his breath in a steady, low whistle. "Well done," he says softly, pushing back his chair.

"Best game I've played all weekend," Randy says.

"In your *life*, you mean." Zeke laughs. No excuses. For the first time, a loss doesn't feel all that deflating. He came back from the dead and beat Pham, he knocked out the number one seed, and he just came within a couple of moves of stalemate against a pretty damn good player, a player he'd all but beaten in that screwed-up game after lunch.

No sore wrist, no momentum killer, just an all-out effort that came up short.

■ ELEVEN ■
Declining Offers

Dina steps out of the bathroom in Randy's hotel room just as he's putting his photo of her into his gym bag. He looks up and says, "Hi."

"Hi." She stands near the door and says, "Big room."

Randy suddenly feels awkward with her, standing between two unmade beds, even though they've been in the room alone for less than two minutes. "Zeke slept here," he says.

"Oh. Because you were lonesome?"

"No."

"*He* was?"

"No. . . . We just got to talking, so he stayed."

Dina's been around enough to know that Randy and Zeke can go months at a time without saying anything but a few hostile words to each other. "He seems nice today," she says.

"He's got the capacity."

"So you two actually *talked?*"

"Incredible, isn't it?"

Randy walks to the bathroom to make sure he hasn't left anything. "I guess that's it," he says. "We need to go."

"Did you guys have *fun?*" Dina asks.

Randy puffs out his cheeks, thinks it over for a second, and decides that they did. "We're going to coach soccer together. Little kids. Can you believe that? Me and him."

"Wow," she says. "Never thought I'd see that. Maybe it won't be two against one all the time anymore."

"What do you mean?"

"Zeke and your father against you."

"Is it that obvious?"

She laughs. "Did you actually think that it wasn't?"

Back in the conference room, Zeke sits next to Dina and turns to his mom. "No sign of Dad?"

"Not lately," she says.

"You think he'll show?"

She frowns and shrugs. "Knowing him, yes. He'll act as if nothing happened. Like he always does."

"He's *killing* us, Mom."

She shrugs. "I guess he is."

"Randy would be okay without him."

"Maybe you should mind your own business, Zeke."

"He can see him every weekend. And I'll . . . keep an

102

eye on Randy." He lowers his voice even further. "Plus, he's got . . . her."

Dina taps Zeke on the shoulder, and he turns, hoping she didn't hear that last comment.

"This guy is really good?" she asks.

"Pramod? He's good. We'll see *how* good. He managed to get through five entire rounds without facing another seeded player, but that's just how it goes sometimes."

"Because he *looks* like an excellent chess player, but he also looks too confident for his own good. . . . Like *you* do sometimes, you know?"

Zeke laughs gently. "You noticed that, huh?"

"You can't really *not* notice that about someone. . . . Sometimes I think maybe Randy's too *nice* for his own good. In chess, I mean."

"He might surprise you. . . . In chess, I mean."

"Yeah. I don't think he could ever be mean in real life."

"No."

"Sarcastic, yeah. But never unkind. Not Randy."

Randy takes his seat and starts setting up the black pieces. Pramod has his white pawns on the board, but apparently he's been waiting for Randy before setting up the others. He picks up a bishop and glances back and forth from it to the board, then puts it in the wrong spot. Then he sets up his other seven pieces incorrectly and waits for Randy to notice.

The door opens, and two adults enter the room. Randy can tell immediately that the man has to be Pramod's father—his skin is a shade darker, but the cut of his jaw and the narrow nose are the same—and the woman, who is white, is probably Pramod's mom. They scurry to the back row and sit down.

"I'm not sure, but I think you've got those horsey things and the castles in the wrong place," Randy says.

"Yeah," Pramod says slowly. He lifts his fist to his jaw, as if he's trying to recall the right positions.

"The championship match will begin in one minute," says Dr. Kerrigan.

Pramod, all business now, fixes the setup and gives Randy a hard stare.

Both players are tentative in the early going, seeking to gain control of the center but not risking any material in doing so.

Randy's been waiting uneasily all afternoon for that door handle to jiggle and his father to slip into the room. They're five minutes into the game when he shows up as predicted, tiptoeing in and hunching low as he walks to the folding chair at the end of the line. As if no one would even notice.

The Regional Director clears his throat but does not look over at Mr. Mansfield.

The corner of Pramod's mouth lifts almost imperceptibly, just enough so he's sure Randy notices.

Randy scowls slightly. He's been pondering whether to slowly build an attack on Pramod's queen or just capture a bishop with a knight. Pramod's smugness pisses him off, so he makes the bolder move and takes the bishop. It's the first advantage either player has taken. On his next move, Randy gets that knight out of harm's way.

Pramod shrugs, as if he's been asked a question.

And Randy does feel more at ease with his father in the

room. Not for emotional support or anything like that, but simply for knowing that the inevitable interruption of his arrival is over.

Randy's felt that same sickening anticipation a lot lately at home, never quite knowing what the guy's mood will be when he walks in the door. He wonders if he really wants three and a half more years of *that*.

The door opens again, and everyone looks up. It's a photographer wearing a tag that says The Scranton Observer. He nods to the Regional Director and begins snapping pictures from several angles, trying to be inconspicuous. Pramod shoots him an angry look, but Randy just ignores him.

Ten minutes later Randy has taken four pawns and lost only three, and he likes the way that he's positioned his two knights and a rook.

Pramod backtracks with his remaining bishop, and Randy's chest wells up slightly, his eyes narrow their focus, and his heart begins to beat a bit faster. He moves his kingside rook forward two spaces, forking one of Pramod's pawns and his queen. Of course, Pramod moves to save his queen, but every little capture helps, and Randy is thrilled to take another pawn.

Aggressive is not a word one would use to describe Randy, but today is different. He steps up his offense and sees things more clearly than ever—three, four, five moves ahead—knowing how Pramod will have to respond to every move and how Randy will capitalize on any waver. Nothing that Pramod does surprises him. Randy soon has nearly twice as many pieces as Pramod.

Eventually Pramod brings his lone knight to a safe position near the center of the board. He raps his knuckles lightly on the table and says, "I offer a draw."

Randy scans the board to see if he's overlooking something, but the advantage is very clearly his. Pramod's just trying to avoid a loss. He tilts his head to the side; says, "I decline"; and attacks that knight with a pawn.

Pramod moves the knight back to where it was, and Randy shifts his queen three spaces along the back rank.

Pramod moves a pawn one space forward and again says, "I offer a draw."

He's got to be kidding, Randy thinks. *I'm two moves away from checkmate*.

Randy doesn't say anything. He declines the draw by shifting his bishop three diagonal spaces forward and looks up at Pramod.

"I've got things to do today," Pramod mutters so only Randy can hear. "No draw, then I resign. What's the big deal? We're both going to the next round anyway."

Yeah, but there's also that little matter of a thousand dollars. The runner-up gets nothing but a plaque and an invitation to Philadelphia. "You resign?"

"I *said*, 'I resign.'"

Randy shakes his head slowly. It's just like Pramod to concede the game without admitting defeat, as if whatever he has to do couldn't wait another two minutes. "Okay," Randy says. He stands up and reaches out his hand.

Pramod shakes it. The spectators applaud politely except for Mr. Mansfield, who claps loudly and whistles.

"What just happened?" Dina asks Zeke.

"We won," Zeke says, beaming. "It was a slaughter."

The Regional Director motions to Randy and shows him a form that he needs to fill out for next weekend's state championship. "One thing to note: We did make an error last night. Anyone under eighteen who elected to stay at the hotel was supposed to have an adult with them in the room."

"No big deal," Randy says. "Right?"

"We'll overlook it. But you'll need to list a guardian on the entry form for Philadelphia."

Randy looks at the form, then at his mother, then at his dad. "An adulteration?" he asks the Director.

"Excuse me?"

"Someone eighteen?"

"Yes."

Randy writes "Zeke Mansfield" on the line. The Regional Director hands him an information sheet for the state championship and wishes him good luck.

"This is fantastic," Mr. Mansfield says, patting Randy on the shoulder as the family gathers in the lobby. "I couldn't be prouder of you guys. First and third out of the very best chess players in this half of the state."

"Nice math, Dad," Zeke says. "There are eight regionals. That's not exactly half."

"Pretty close. Here, I got you something when I was over at the mall." He hands a shopping bag to Zeke.

Zeke takes out a new sleeve of bright yellow tennis balls. "Thanks," he says flatly.

"And as if you need any more awards," Mr. Mansfield says, beaming at Randy and handing him the other bag, "see how you like this."

Randy opens the bag and takes out a slim paperback book:

101 Tips for Young Chess Champions. He nods and says, "Thanks." It's a book Randy could have written.

"Technically I *tied* for third with Serena," Zeke says. "They didn't have a consolation round."

"Believe me, you would have beat her. Let's call it third."

"Let's call it a tie," Zeke says, looking away. "It is what it is, right?"

"If they'd set up the brackets better, you two would have met in the final and you'd *both* be going to Philly," Mr. Mansfield says. "Either one of you would have knocked off that Indian kid. That was obvious."

"It was, huh?"

"It was to me. But what do you expect? That idiot running this thing doesn't seem to know his ass from his elbow."

"He was all right," Zeke says. "He tried to be fair."

"My ass he did. He totally screwed you in that semifinal. Interrupting the game like that."

Randy looks at Zeke, who has a familiar look of disbelief. They both know where this is going. You can't keep playing a game nobody can win.

"Anyway," Mr. Mansfield says, "that's all behind us now. No sense dwelling on something somebody else did to us."

"That's the spirit," Zeke says.

"That's right," Mr. Mansfield says, missing Zeke's obvious sarcasm. "We're bigger than that. Let that wimp-ass have his 'rules.' We've got the trophy. We . . . kicked . . . butt!"

He goes outside for a cigarette. Pramod and his parents have come out of the conference room, and they all shake Randy's hand.

"You played really well all weekend," Pramod says, turning off his jerk switch in front of his parents. "See you in Philly."

"I'll be there."

Mrs. Mansfield is talking to Jenna's parents, so Jenna walks over to Zeke and Randy. Dina, sitting alone on the couch, gets up and follows Jenna.

"So," Jenna says to Dina, "I guess I might see you this week?"

"Really?"

Zeke says, "Yeah," sort of excitedly, aiming the word at Dina. "I thought you guys might want to go to a basketball game. . . . It's at Jenna's school."

"Oh." Dina gives a confused smile. "Because if it's Thursday, I *might* be going to my friend Becky's house if we have a project due on Friday for biology. But I *think* it's not due until the week after next, but I have to check to make sure."

"The game's on Tuesday."

"Tuesday's good! The project definitely isn't due until after that."

"Well," Randy says dryly, tapping a finger on his new chess book, "I've got some heavy-duty reading to do if I've got any chance of winning in Philadelphia. So we'll see you Tuesday."

Dina and Randy walk toward his mom. Zeke and Jenna stay behind briefly.

"Ready to go?" Mrs. Mansfield asks.

"Absolutely," Randy says.

"We've got two cars here."

"I know."

Mr. Mansfield has already pulled his car up to the loading

area in front of the hotel. The car is running, but he's standing outside it, finishing his smoke.

"Not a bad day," he says as Randy and Dina and his wife walk by on the way to her car. "Quite a day to be a Mansfield."

Randy nods seriously and Dina smiles, but all three of them keep walking.

"I'll just wait for Zeke," Mr. Mansfield says, ignoring the snub.

Randy stops on the sidewalk and waits a few seconds until Zeke comes out. Dina and Mrs. Mansfield get in her car.

"Hop in," Randy hears his father say to Zeke.

Zeke stops for a second, looks at his dad, and points his thumb toward the others. "I'll ride with them," he says. "We've got some things to talk about."

"Suit yourself, Ace," Mr. Mansfield says. He gets in the car and pulls the door shut, flicking his cigarette butt out the window. "I'll see you all back at the house."

Randy's stomach tightens, and his eyes start to sting. Zeke catches up and says, "What are you crying about?"

"I'm *not* crying."

Zeke looks away and balls his hands into fists, then lets out a sigh. He puts a fist gently on Randy's back, between the shoulder blades, and whispers, "He's gotta go. You know it, too."

Randy wipes at one eye and nods.

"You were the best, no question," Zeke says.

"And you *were* better than Pramod," Randy replies. "Dad was right about that one."

"Yeah, but he was right in the wrong way. Like always. You

play the hand you're dealt. If I'd been playing Pramod in the semi instead of you, then I *would* have got disqualified when Dad opened his mouth."

"Maybe. But maybe he would have kept his mouth shut."

Zeke gives a scornful laugh. "He doesn't know how. He picks on you, he picks on Mom. And he gets worse every day. We all know it."

They stand on the sidewalk for a few more seconds until their mother pulls up. Randy gets in the back next to Dina. She's holding his trophy. It's about fifteen inches tall with a gold-tinted king on top and a circle of pawns around it.

They pull out of the lot, onto Jefferson, and head for the Central Scranton Expressway.

"Mr. Chess," Dina says, lifting the trophy.

"Careful with that," Randy says. "It needs to stay intact for the parade."

"What parade?"

"The giant celebration in my honor back in town."

"Oh. That one."

"Yeah. Zeke's arranging it, right?"

Zeke smiles. "Absolutely. Got it all planned. A giant parade-ulation on Main Street."

"Can I be in it?" Dina asks.

"Of course," Randy says. "You'll ride on the big float with me."

They all laugh, but then things turn quiet. Randy scoots closer to Dina, and she leans her head on his shoulder. The drive back to Sturbridge will take about thirty-five minutes. Plenty of time to talk things out.

Zeke clears his throat and turns to face Randy. "You can handle this, right? You're ready?"

Randy thinks for a moment. He locks his eyes on Zeke's, and for the first time in his life, he sees something positive there. Support, maybe. Trust.

"Yeah, I'm ready," Randy replies. "We all are."

RICH WALLACE is the acclaimed author of *Wrestling Sturbridge*, an ALA Top Ten Best Book for Young Adults; *Shots on Goal*, a *Booklist* Top 10 Youth Sports Book; *Playing Without the Ball*, an ALA Quick Pick; *Losing Is Not an Option*; and *One Good Punch*, an ALA Best Book for Young Adults. He grew up in a small town in northern New Jersey where competitive sports were a way of life. Since then he's worked as a sports-writer, a news editor, and a magazine editor. Rich Wallace lives in Pennsylvania with his wife and two sons.